MATT & TOM OLDFIELD

CLASSIC
FOOTBALL HER●ES

# ÁLVAREZ

FROM THE PLAYGROUND
TO THE PITCH

DINO

First published by Dino Books in 2024,
an imprint of Bonnier Books UK,
4th Floor, Victoria House, Bloomsbury Square, London WC1B 4DA
Owned by Bonnier Books,
Sveavägen 56, Stockholm, Sweden

X @UFHbooks
X @footieheroesbks
www.heroesfootball.com
www.bonnierbooks.co.uk

Text © Matt Oldfield 2024

Paperback ISBN: 978 1 78946 794 9
E-book ISBN: 978 1 78946 788 8

British Library cataloguing-in-publication data:
A catalogue record for this book is available from the British Library.

Printed and bound in Great Britain by Clays Ltd, Elcograf S.p.A.

1 3 5 7 9 10 8 6 4 2

MIX
Paper | Supporting
responsible forestry
FSC
www.fsc.org
FSC® C018072

# ÁLVAREZ

*For Noah, Nico, Arlo and Lila*

CLASSIC
FOOTBALL HEROES

Matt Oldfield is a children's author focusing on the wonderful world of football. His other books include *Unbelievable Football* (winner of the 2020 Children's Sports Book of the Year) and the *Johnny Ball: Football Genius* series. In association with his writing, Matt also delivers writing workshops in schools.

Cover illustration by Dan Leydon.
To learn more about Dan, visit danleydon.com
To purchase his artwork visit etsy.com/shop/footynews
Or just follow him on X @danleydon

# TABLE OF CONTENTS

# ACKNOWLEDGEMENTS

First of all I'd like to thank everyone at Bonnier Books for supporting me and for running the ever-expanding UFH ship so smoothly. Writing stories for the next generation of football fans is both an honour and a pleasure. Thanks also to my agent, Nick Walters, for helping to keep my dream job going, year after year.

Next up, an extra big cheer for all the teachers, booksellers and librarians who have championed these books, and, of course, for the readers. The success of this series is truly down to you.

Okay, onto friends and family. I wouldn't be writing this series if it wasn't for my brother Tom. I owe him so much and I'm very grateful for his belief in me as an author. I'm also very grateful to the rest of my family, especially Mel, Noah, Nico, and of course Mum and Dad. To my parents, I owe my biggest passions: football and books. They're a real inspiration for everything I do.

## CHAPTER 1

# ARGENTINA'S WORLD CUP WONDER

*13 December 2022, Lusail Iconic Stadium, Qatar*

As the two teams walked out of the tunnel and onto the pitch, the noise of the crowd was deafening. Wow – what an amazing atmosphere, and what a spectacular sight as well: a mass of red and white checks for Croatia, and then a much bigger, wider sea of sky-blue and white Argentina shirts, flags and scarves. Julián was already feeling pumped up for the semi-final ahead, but now his heart was pounding faster than ever.

'Let's do this!' he called out to his teammate, Enzo Fernández, while they lined up together for the national anthems. Both youngsters had begun the tournament on the bench for Argentina, but since then, they had shown the spirit and skill to force their way into the starting line-up.

So now, at the age of just twenty-two, Julián was already living all his childhood dreams at once:

To play for his country – *Tick!*

To play at a World Cup – *Tick!*

To play alongside his hero, Lionel Messi – *Tick!*

Unbelievable! Lionel was still the captain and star of the Argentina team, of course, but now he had a talented young second striker to play alongside him. With his hard work and powerful runs, Julián had won the hearts of the fans, and with his goals, he had also won games for Argentina.

His right-foot rocket against Poland had helped get them through the group stage, and then in the Round of 16 against Australia, Julián had raced in to pounce on the keeper's mistake and score a crucial second goal for Argentina:

1–0 – a moment of Messi magic,

2–0 – a moment of Álvarez aggression.

Yes, Lionel and Julián looked the real deal, the perfect partnership. Now, what could they do together in the World Cup semi-finals against Croatia?

It took Argentina twenty minutes to really get going, but once they did, they looked dangerous every time they attacked.

First, Lionel played a lovely one-two with Julián and then almost threaded a perfect pass through to Enzo. *So close!*

Then Enzo fired a curling shot towards the bottom corner, which the Croatia keeper, Dominik Livaković, dived down to save. *Nearly!*

'Keep going, a goal is coming!' captain Lionel cried, urging his Argentina teammates on.

He was right. In the thirty-second minute, Enzo robbed the ball off Luka Modrić on the halfway line and quickly launched a long pass down the middle, not for Lionel, but for Julián...

*ZOOM!* He was off, chasing after the ball at top speed, bursting past the Croatia centre-backs with ease. This was it; a golden chance to score again for Argentina. Julián was into the penalty area now and one-on-one with Livaković, but as he tried to chip the ball round him, the keeper knocked him to the ground.

*Heyyyyy!* As he lay sprawled out on the grass, Julián turned to look back at the referee. Surely that was a foul and a penalty?

The answer was yes, and up stepped Lionel to give Argentina the lead. *1–0!*

Right, now that they were winning, was it time to calm down, stay back, and see things through to half-time? No, that wasn't Julián's style at all. He never stopped. Five minutes later, he raced in bravely to block a Croatia cross, and then watched with growing excitement as Enzo nodded the ball down to Lionel, who flicked it on to… Julián!

*ZOOM!* He was off again, this time on the counterattack, with the ball at his feet! As he burst forward over the halfway line, Julián had three defenders around him, but on he went, charging his way past them, one by one. Yes, he got a little lucky along the way, but at the end of it all, Julián showed the skill and composure to chest the ball down and finish on the volley. *2–0!*

*Goooooooooooooooooooaaaaaaaaaaaaaaaalllllllllllllll llllllllllll!!!!!!!!!!!!!!!!!!!!!*

Woah, what a wonderful, powerful run, and in a World Cup semi-final! As Julián jogged over to the corner flag to celebrate, he was surrounded by excited teammates, but who was the very first player to run over and hug him? Yes, his captain, strike partner and childhood hero, Lionel!

'VAMOOOOOOOOOS!' they cheered together.

It was a moment that Julián would never forget, but he didn't stop there. No – he never stopped and he always wanted more. So, in the second half, when Lionel skipped away from his marker and raced up the right wing, Julián didn't just stand back and watch; he followed him all the way.

When Lionel dribbled into the box, the Croatia defenders thought they had him surrounded, but no, it was time for some more Messi magic. He twisted and turned his way past Joško Gvardiol again, before pulling the ball back for… Julián! With a swing of his right leg, he swept it into the net. *3–0!*

*Goooooooooooooooooooaaaaaaaaaaaaaaaalllllllllllll llllllllllll!!!!!!!!!!!!!!!!!!!!!*

Julián had his second goal of the semi-final, but this time, the hard work had been done by someone else. So, he rushed straight over to throw his arms around his awesome strike partner. Together, they were crushing Croatia and making their country proud.

'Thanks, Leo – you're the best!'

They still had twenty-five minutes left to play. Finally, when the match was over, it was official: Argentina were through to the 2022 World Cup final!

'Yesssssssssssssssssss!' By then, Julián was taking a well-earned rest on the substitutes' bench, but he rushed straight back on to the pitch to join in the joyful team celebrations. What a night, and what a feeling!

Later on, Lionel was named Man of the Match, but in his speech, he asked to give the prize to his strike partner instead. 'Every player did very well, but if I have to choose I would give this award to Julián. He had an extraordinary game,' the Argentina captain said. 'He paved the way for us.'

Wow, those were amazing words to hear from your ultimate hero, and that wasn't all. Julián had also just become the youngest player to score two goals in a World Cup semi-final since a certain Brazilian superstar, way back in 1958. Yes, Pelé!

From kickarounds with his brothers to shining on football's biggest stage – what an incredible journey it had been so far for the Little Spider of Calchín, and Julián was still only just getting started.

## CHAPTER 2

# THE LITTLE SPIDER
# OF CALCHÍN

'Hey, we're going out to play on the pitch – wanna join?'

As a young boy, little Julián heard his older brothers, Rafael and Agustin, ask that question so many times, and yet it never failed to make him smile and send a shiver of excitement down his spine. Oh, and his answer was always the same:

'Yes, coming, wait for me!'

'The pitch' that his brothers were talking about wasn't something big or beautiful, but it didn't need to be. Calchín, the place where they lived in central Argentina, was a tiny town of only 3,000 people, and it was mostly known for farming, not football. There were never that many kids who wanted to play, and that's partly why Rafael and Agustin were always so keen to bring their little brother along.

But despite the rocks, rubbish and rusted goalposts, 'the pitch' still offered the kids of Calchín exactly what they wanted: enough space to live out their football fantasies.

'Right, let's play – I'll be Saviola!'

'Ok, but I'm Aimar!'

'And I'm Riquelme.'

'Fiiiiiiine, who's left? I guess I'll be Mascherano then!'

Inspired by their Argentina national team heroes, their games would often go on for hours and hours, especially during the summer holidays. Because why stop for anything other than dinner or darkness? They were having so much football fun!

In his early days at the pitch, Julián was usually the smallest and the youngest player there, but he never let that stop him. He already loved everything about the game of football – tackling, passing, dribbling, shooting, even heading – and he was determined to be the best player on the pitch one day. So he ran and ran all over the field, bravely chasing after the ball as fast as his little legs would carry him.

*'Unlucky, Julián – keep going!'*

By the age of four, Julián was a bit bigger, a bit stronger, and his football skills were a lot better. In fact, he had become so good at dribbling speedily with the ball that everything was a blur, especially his dancing feet. It sometimes seemed as though Julián had more than two legs.

'Woah, look at him, he's like a little Spider!' one of his brothers said one day, and that was it, the nickname stuck straight away. '*El Aranita*', The Little Spider.

'I love it!' Julián thought to himself proudly as the three Álvarez brothers walked home together. All of their favourite footballers had nicknames:

Argentina's exciting young striker Javier Saviola was called '*El Conejo*' – 'The Rabbit',

Their playmaker Pablo Aimar was '*El Mago*' – 'The Wizard',

Midfield maestro Juan Román Riquelme was '*El Torero*' – 'The Bullfighter',

Defensive midfielder Javier Mascherano was '*El Jefecito*' – 'The Little Chief',

And soon, hopefully, there would be a new nickname to add to that superstar list...

The Little Spider!

Really? Why not?! It was always good to dream big, and it wasn't as if Julián would be Calchín's first ever international footballer. No, instead he would be the second, after a man called Germán Martellotto. Martellotto was a creative midfielder who had played one match for Argentina back in 1991, but what a match it was: a 2–2 draw with England at the world-famous Wembley Stadium.

Gary Lineker's goal, Diego Simeone's tough tackling – Julián had heard all about that game because his father, Gustavo, was friends with Germán, and Julián was friends with Germán's son, Federico. Yes, Calchín was one of those small towns where everyone knew each other.

So, would Julián be the one to follow in Germán's inspiring footsteps? Could The Little Spider of Calchín go all the way from the local pitch to the highest level?

Only time would tell, but by then, his journey to the top had already begun, playing for the only football club in town.

## CHAPTER 3

# THE "CRACK" OF ATLÉTICO CALCHÍN

Rafael Varas, the coach of Atlético Calchín, had actually first spotted Julián when he was only two years old. At the time, Rafael and Agustin were both already training at the club, so of course their younger brother was there as well, desperately wanting to do the same.

'Look at his little legs go!' Varas laughed to himself as he watched the tiny boy race across the pitch after a ball that was almost as big as him. But when he reached the ball and started kicking it around, that laughter soon turned to surprise. Wow, the kid was incredible! For his age, he controlled the ball beautifully and he could kick powerfully and accurately too.

'What a wonderful player he could be!' Varas thought to himself excitedly.

Sadly, Julián wasn't old enough to sign up straight away, but eventually, at the age of three-and-a-half, he officially became an Atlético Calchín player.

What a proud moment! Not only was he joining his brothers at the club, but Julián was also starting out on his own amazing football adventure. Who knew where it might take him – to other countries, to major international tournaments, maybe even to Europe? But before all that, Julián had big dreams to achieve at home in Argentina. First things first, he wanted to shine in the shirt of Atlético Calchín: white with a red diagonal stripe across the middle. Beautiful!

'Looking good, Little Spider!' Julián declared proudly, as he admired himself in the hallway mirror. He couldn't wait to wear it out on the pitch one day, the proper pitch in the club's proper stadium, which even had seats for 150 supporters to watch him score.

Varas couldn't wait for that day either, and he had no doubt that the Little Spider would shine. Just as the

Atlético coach had predicted, when Julián joined the team, he immediately became their best player. Right from his very first practice session, he stood out high above the rest in every area of the game.

He worked harder than everyone else,

He ran faster than everyone else,

He dribbled the ball better than everyone else,

And he kicked it harder than everyone else.

That was true in training, and it was true once their league matches started too. Against other local teams, Julián scored goal after goal for Atlético, leading them to victory after victory. Sometimes, he weaved his way through entire defences with his dancing feet, and other times, he fired off unstoppable shots from long distance. On one extra-special occasion, he even scored with a Rabona shot! Julián could do it all, and the more he did, the more people started talking about his talent.

'Is the Little Spider playing today?' referees and opposition coaches would ask as soon as they arrived at the Atlético stadium. 'I heard he's the best young player Calchín has ever seen, and he's destroying everyone!'

In the early days, Varas just smiled and shrugged his shoulders, but after a while, he didn't even try to deny it. 'Yeah, that kid is going to be a crack!' he replied with confidence, even when Julián was still only six years old.

In South America, a 'crack' was a football superstar who had the best skills and scored the best goals. The legendary Diego Maradona had been Argentina's original crack, followed by a long line of 'New Maradonas': Ariel Ortega, Riquelme, Saviola, Aimar, all the way through to the country's latest wonderkid, Lionel Messi.

Wow, and what a crack Lionel was! From the moment Julián first saw Messi on TV playing for Barcelona, he had a new favourite football hero.

'The guy's an absolute genius!' he kept telling his brothers, who soon grew bored of hearing about him.

If Messi was 'the new Maradona', could Julián be 'the new Messi'? The older he got and the more goals he scored for his team, the more he began to think seriously about his football future. Sure, he was having lots of fun being the crack of Atlético Calchín for now, but what if one day he could become the crack of a bigger club, like… River Plate?

They were Julián's favourite team in Argentina, as well as the home club of Aimar and Saviola, and they even wore the same kit colours as Atlético Calchín. A white shirt with a red diagonal stripe across the middle – beautiful!

'See, it's meant to be!' he argued passionately with his brothers.

By the age of eleven, however, Julián was dreaming even higher than River Plate. Just like his hero Messi, it looked as if he might be moving to Spain, to play for one of Europe's biggest clubs.

## CHAPTER 4

# READY FOR... REAL MADRID?

'Real Madrid? REAL MADRID?'

Julián had to repeat the words several times because he couldn't believe what he was hearing. Real Madrid were one of the most famous football clubs in the world, with a long history of glory and superstars like Raúl, Roberto Carlos, Luís Figo, David Beckham, Zinedine Zidane, and Cristiano Ronaldo. Surely this had to be either a mistake or a really bad joke?

'Yes, Real Madrid!' Gustavo told his son for a second time with a nod and a wide smile. 'I know it's a big deal and a lot to take in, but they want you to come over to Spain and play for them in a tournament.'

What?! Really?!

'Me?' Julián was still struggling to accept the amazing news. 'How does a big club like that even know who I am?'

The answer to that question was a man called Piero Foglia. Foglia's main job was manager of a team called Club Deportivo Atalaya in the city of Córdoba. Córdoba was more than an hour's drive away from Calchín, but word was already spreading far and wide about Atlético's young crack.

'Have you heard of that kid they're calling The Little Spider?' asked one of Foglia's friends, who worked as a referee. 'Julián Álvarez – he plays for Atlético Calchín and he's incredible!'

Hmmm, interesting! 'Thanks,' Foglia replied, making sure to remember the name. You see, alongside his coaching job, he also worked as a scout for the Argentina national youth teams, so he was always on the hunt for the next big thing. 'Maybe I'll go and take a look at him.'

'Seriously, you really should – he's going to be a superstar!'

Foglia's friend was right. When he travelled to

Calchín to watch Julián in action, he spotted his special talent straight away. For someone so young, his all-round game was excellent, from his perfect control to his clever passing. And it wasn't just the boy's skills *on* the ball that impressed him; it was also his hard work *off* the ball. Whether he was tracking back to make a tackle or sprinting forward into space, he never stopped running for his team.

'He certainly doesn't act like an arrogant little superstar,' Foglia thought to himself, 'and he's definitely got that winner's mindset...'

Within a few minutes, he could see that Julián was far too good to stay at Atlético Calchín forever, but where should he go next? To one of the two biggest clubs in Argentina perhaps, Boca Juniors or River Plate? Or what about... Real Madrid?

Foglia knew their Sporting Director, Ramón Martínez, and when they met up in 2011, Martínez asked him if there were any young local players that he would recommend. Oh yes, Foglia had a name for him:

'Julián Álvarez.'

And so now the Little Spider was on his way from Argentina to Spain! Even though Julián was a big fan of their rivals Barcelona (because of Messi, of course), he couldn't say no to a huge club like Real Madrid. What an opportunity! He would be representing them in the Peralanda tournament, a youth competition taking place in the city of Girona.

A trial for a top team in a totally new country, 10,000 miles from home – most eleven-year-olds would have found the whole idea pretty terrifying, but Julián didn't see it that way. What was there to worry about? He just saw it as an exciting chance to play football, test himself against some of Europe's best young players, and hopefully win a trophy. That sounded fun, not nerve-wracking!

*Vamooooooooooos!*

When the tournament kicked off, Julián stayed calm and scored twice to help send Real Madrid through to the final. The club's youth coaches were already very impressed, but Little Spider had saved his biggest moment for the biggest match of all. With his team drawing 0–0 with Real Betis in the final, it was Julián who made the difference by setting up the crucial opening goal.

*'What a pass – we've got to sign him up!'*

When the final whistle blew, Real Madrid were the winners, and Julián danced around the pitch with his teammates, and the trophy in his hands. What a feeling! He was having the time of his life at Real Madrid, but as his trial week came to a successful end, the big question was: would he be staying in Spain for good?

Julián really hoped so, both for himself and for his family. If he signed for Real Madrid, he would be following in the footsteps of his hero Messi, who moved from Argentina to Barcelona aged thirteen. Plus, if he signed, his parents wouldn't have to worry about money anymore. Back in Calchín, they worked long hours for fairly low pay – his dad Gustavo in an office and his mum Mariana in an infant school – but suddenly they would be free to do whatever they wanted in Madrid.

The Álvarez family crossed their fingers and hoped for the best, but sadly, Julián's Spanish dream did not come true. Despite Real's best efforts to get the deal done, unfortunately the FIFA rules had changed since the days of Messi's move. Now, clubs could only sign young players from foreign countries if they were at least sixteen years old.

Sixteen? Noooooooooooo! To an eleven-year-old like Julián, that was a very long time to wait. So, with a heavy heart, he travelled back home to Argentina, to carry on playing at Atlético Calchín. For now.

## CHAPTER 5

# MAD ABOUT MESSI

It took Julián a few weeks to recover from his Real Madrid disappointment, but with time, he began to wonder if maybe it was for the best, after all. Was he really ready to leave his home behind and start again across the world in Spain? The answer was... no. Not yet, anyway.

Okay, well what about signing for one of Argentina's top teams instead? That same year, Julián travelled to his country's capital city, Buenos Aires, for trials at River Plate, the club that he supported, and at Boca Juniors too. But while they were both interesting experiences that he really enjoyed, in the end, Julián decided not to commit his future to either club.

'Thank you very much for the opportunity,' he told them politely, 'but I'm not ready to make up my mind.'

Turning down big opportunities like that was certainly a risky thing to do. What if he didn't get another chance – would Julián one day regret his decision? Perhaps, but what was the rush? He was still only eleven years old, so he would wait until the timing felt right. For now, he wanted to stay in Calchín with his family and friends, just playing football for fun…

As the ball bounced down inside the penalty area, Julián pounced in a flash, blasting a curling shot past the keeper.

*Goooooooooooooooooooooaaaaaaaaaaaaaaaaalllllllllllllll llllllllllllll!!!!!!!!!!!!!!!!!!!!!*

'Yesssssssss, Little Spider – what a strike!'

Collecting the ball near the halfway line, he turned and dribbled forward at full speed. He skipped past one defender, then another, then in between two more, before calmly placing the ball in the bottom corner.

*Goooooooooooooooooooooaaaaaaaaaaaaaaaalllllllllllllll llllllllllllll!!!!!!!!!!!!!!!!!!!!!!*

'Woah, how on earth did you do that, Julián?'

Being the local superstar wasn't all goals and glory, though. The older he got and the brighter he shone, the more his opponents tried everything they could to stop him: kicking him, pushing him, pulling his shirt, calling him rude names…

'Hey, come on, ref!' Varas often shouted angrily from the sidelines. 'That's a clear foul – are you just going to let them get away with that all game long?'

But no matter what happened to him out on the pitch, Julián never lost his cool. What was the point in fighting with defenders or arguing with referees? That wasn't going to help his team to win. Instead, it was much better to let his dancing feet do the talking…

Julián used his surprising strength to hold off the big centre-back and then his skill to flick the ball through his legs. Nutmeg! Julián was away, racing past a reckless flying tackle and towards the opposition box. When he got there, he unleashed a powerful low shot, leaving the keeper with no chance.

*Goooooooooooooooooooaaaaaaaaaaaaaaaallllllllllllll llllllllllll!!!!!!!!!!!!!!!!!!!!!*

'You did it – we won the league thanks to you!'

'No, WE did it together!'

*Campeones, Campeones, Olé! Olé! Olé!*

Atlético's humble hero was loving life back in Calchín, but he definitely wasn't giving up on achieving his bigger goals. No, Julián still wanted to be a famous professional crack one day, and when he was interviewed for a club video about all things football, his answers were the same as always:

What's your dream in football?

'To play at a World Cup.'

Who's your idol?

'Messi.'

Yes, an Argentina strikeforce of Álvarez and Messi – that was the aim.

If anything, Julián was now madder about Messi than ever. When he wasn't trying to copy his skills and free kicks on the football pitch, he was watching everything he could find about him at home: interviews, training clips, highlight videos, plus loads of live Barcelona and Argentina matches on TV.

'You're obsessed! There are other top footballers out there, you know,' his brothers liked to tease him. Why would Julián want to watch anyone else, though?

Messi had already won five Spanish league titles, three Champions League trophies, plus four Ballon d'Or awards in a row – what a superstar! He had always been a brilliant player, but by 2012, he had become the best in the world, and maybe even the greatest footballer EVER. Julián certainly thought so, and when Messi returned to Argentina to play a match for the national team, he was desperate to meet him. But when, where and how?

Proudly wearing his sky-blue and white striped Argentina shirt, Julián waited and waited at the players' hotel until finally, Messi walked past.

GULP! What should he do now? What should he say? This was his big chance to speak to his hero; it was now or never. Clearing his throat, Julián plucked up the courage to ask, 'Err, can I get a picture with you please?'

'Sure,' Argentina's superstar replied, stopping just

behind Julián's left shoulder.

FLASH!

'Thanks... g-good luck!'

It wasn't the best of photos – Messi looked a bit grumpy – but that really didn't matter. What mattered was that Julián had met his ultimate football hero and he had a souvenir of that unforgettable moment.

Although it turned out Julián would have plenty more unforgettable moments with Messi ahead...

## CHAPTER 6

# READY FOR... RIVER PLATE!

In 2015, a man called Alfredo Alonso arrived at a youth tournament near Córdoba, looking for Argentina's next great goalkeeper. That's what his team, Argentinos Juniors, had asked him to find, but what the scout found instead was Argentina's next great goal*scorer*.

Well, actually, scoring goals was only one part of what this wonderkid could do. He was able to play all over the pitch, and so that's what he did.

Sometimes, he dropped deep into midfield and then played clever passes through to the other attackers. *GOAL!*

Sometimes, he went out wide as a winger

and then dribbled infield, weaving his way past defenders. *GOAL!*

And sometimes, he moved around the penalty area like a striker, always alert and ready to pounce. *GOAL!*

'Wow, he's amazing!' Alonso marvelled, completely forgetting about his goalkeeper search. That could wait; right now, he had to find out who this fantastic forward was.

'Oh, that's Julián Álvarez,' one of the coaches at the tournament told him. 'They call him The Little Spider.'

The Little Spider, eh? Alonso liked the nickname a lot, and he liked the player it belonged to even more. It was a long time since he'd scouted a kid with so much 'crack' potential. He couldn't wait to get back to Buenos Aires and tell everyone at Argentinos Juniors about him.

'I've found us a future superstar!' Alonso announced at the next team meeting. 'The only problem is he lives in Calchín, so do you think we could pay for him to come here for a week's trial?'

Unfortunately, the answer was no. Despite being the first club of Diego Maradona, Argentinos Juniors were not one of the country's richest clubs. They could hardly afford to pay their senior players, so travel and accommodation for a fifteen-year-old kid they knew nothing about? No way!

Alonso nodded glumly at the news, but he wasn't going to give up that easily. Oh well, if Argentinos wouldn't pay, then maybe another, richer club would…

'Hey, I've got this great young player I want to talk to you about,' Alonso told his good friend Gabriel Rodríguez, who worked as a scout for River Plate, a club with a lot more money to spend. 'Julián Álvarez is his name, and he's a forward from Calchín. Argentinos won't pay for a trial, but I promise you, this kid is a CRACK!'

Hmmm, interesting! 'Okay, thanks Alfredo,' Rodriguez replied. 'Leave it with me.'

The River Plate scout had an amazing record of discovering Argentina's top young talents: Marcelo Gallardo, Hernán Crespo, Pablo Zabaleta, Érik Lamela… The list went on and on. But an important part of finding future stars was trusting the smart people around you. Alfredo knew what he was talking about, so if he said that this kid was a 'crack', then Rodríguez believed him. It was definitely worth taking a look at him.

'Mr Álvarez, my name is Gabriel Rodríguez and I'm a scout for River Plate,' he explained on a phone call a few days later. 'I'm calling about your son, Julián. We've seen that he's a very talented young player, and we'd like to offer him a week's trial at the club. We'll pay for everything – travel, accommodation, food. What do you think?'

'Thank you, it's a very interesting offer,' Gustavo answered. 'I'll need to speak to Julián about this.'

He was trying to sound as calm and professional as possible, but on the inside, he was jumping for joy. River were giving his son a second chance!

'Of course, yes, just let me know when you're ready,' Rodríguez reassured him before ending the call. 'I look forward to hearing from you.'

So, four years on from his last visit to his favourite football club, how would Julián feel about returning?

'YES!' was his eager response when his dad told

him about the trial. Now, at the age of fifteen, the timing seemed right. Julián was ready to step out of his comfort zone in Calchín and take on a new challenge. He was ready for River Plate.

Julián had always supported the club, through the good times and the bad. Back in 2011, the year of his last trial, the team had been relegated from Argentina's top division for the first time ever. It was a terrible time, but fortunately, they had bounced straight back up, thanks to goals from Fernando Cavenaghi and French striker David Trezeguet, and by 2014, River had become Champions of Argentina again. What a turnaround, what a team! Julián couldn't wait to go back, and hopefully, become a club hero there one day.

'Okay great, I'll let them know!' his dad said with a smile of clear delight.

'Mr Rodríguez, hello it's Gustavo Álvarez here. I've spoken to Julián and he would love to accept your offer. How soon would you like us to come?'

'As soon as possible,' the scout replied.

So, off they went to Buenos Aires, and once the

trial began, Julián got straight to work, racing around the pitch and chasing after every pass. This was his big chance to show what he could do and he was determined to take it.

'Yesssssss!' Julián called out for the ball and when it came, he passed it on quickly and then kept running for the one-two. When he got the ball back, he dribbled forward like a man on a mission, and then with an extra burst of speed, *ZOOM!* he was away, leaving the last defender trailing behind. He was into the box, with just the keeper to beat. The hardest part was over; now, he just needed to stay calm and score…

*Goooooooooooooooooooaaaaaaaaaaaaaaaalllllllllllllll llllllllllll!!!!!!!!!!!!!!!!!!!*

Watching on the sidelines, it only took Rodríguez ten minutes to make his decision. The kid could score goals, and he could create them too, and he understood the game in a way that not many fifteen-year-olds did. Every time he got the ball, he always seemed to know where his teammates were and what to do next. Yes, Julián had what it took to be a

River star.

'Thanks, Alfredo – he *is* a CRACK!'

By the end of the trial, Julián had another offer and an even bigger decision to make. Was he ready to leave home and move 400 miles east to chase his football dream at the club he loved most?

'YES!' was his eager response. After years of wondering and waiting, his moment had arrived. It was Julián's time to shine at River Plate.

## CHAPTER 7

# STRUGGLING TO STAND OUT

Saviola had made his River Plate debut at the age of sixteen, and so had Aimar. Julián was really hoping to shine brightly like his heroes and race through the academy to the first team, but it didn't quite work out that way.

One reason for that was River already had a squad full of talented forwards with a lot more experience: Rodrigo Mora, Rafael Santos Borré, Lucas Alario, plus their latest homegrown star, Sebastián Driussi. So, why would they need a teenage wonderkid?

But another important reason was that Julián simply wasn't ready. He was only just arriving at the club at the age of sixteen, and so of course it was going to take him time to settle in. Everything about River was a massive step-up from Atlético Calchín: the facilities, the coaching, and most of all, the quality of his teammates.

At Atlético, Julián had got used to being the club's only 'crack', the superstar who scored the most goals and stood out high above the rest. But now at River, there were really gifted players all over the pitch, in every position:

Goalkeeper Leo Díaz,

Determined defenders like Elías López,

Stylish midfielders like Tomás Galván and Hernán López Muñoz,

Awesome attackers like Matías Benítez and Benjamín Rollheiser…

And that was just in his own age group – in the years above and below, there were a whole load more. So, how was Julián going to stand out from the talented crowd and fire his way to the River first team?

'One step at a time,' he told himself, starting with the subs bench.

That's where the youth team coach, Juanjo Borrelli,

put Julián at first, but he didn't complain. No problem, he would just have to prove himself as a super sub...

From the moment he came on, Julián never stopped moving. *ZOOM!* He raced around the pitch, chasing every ball and putting pressure on every defender, and even the goalkeeper. All he needed was one mistake or one half-chance, and *BANG!... GOAL!*

'Boy, he must be a nightmare to play against!' Borrelli smiled to himself.

As well as his endless energy, the River coach was also impressed by Julián's super skills. His passing was clever and creative, he was comfortable with both feet, and he could shoot with real power and swerve. Yes, Borrelli could already tell that the boy was going to be a brilliant addition to the team.

'Keep up the good work, kid,' he told Julián, 'and you'll get your chance to start.'

'Thanks, Coach – I will!'

Soon, it was time for the first '*Superclásico*' of the season. River Plate vs Boca Juniors was the greatest rivalry in Argentinian football and Julián was desperate to play his part. He wasn't going to let anything stop him, not even illness.

On the morning of the big match, Julián woke up feeling really unwell, but he didn't tell his manager. No way, he would make him miss the game! So instead, he sat quietly on the subs bench, drinking lots of water and trying to make himself feel a bit better.

At half-time, the game was tied at 1–1, so Borrelli decided to make a change. 'Juli, get warmed up – you're coming on!'

'Yes, Coach!' he replied, hiding his sick feeling behind a smile.

At first, even running a few metres felt like a real effort, but Julián did his best to push through the pain and get himself into the game. This was the Superclásico and his team needed a hero.

'Yessss!' he called out in the middle once he'd moved into space, but instead, River's right winger sent the ball floating high over his head, towards another teammate at the back post.

'Never mind.' Although Julián felt frustrated, he didn't stand there with his arms in the air, complaining. No, he stayed alert and kept running across the box because you never knew what might happen next…

At the back post, the River forward managed to win the header, flicking the ball out towards the edge of the area for… Julián! As it rolled towards him, he took a moment to calm himself and then *BANG!* he struck his shot first time, catching everyone by surprise. The ball flew in between two defenders, past the diving keeper, and into the corner of the net. *2–1!*

*Goooooooooooooooooooooaaaaaaaaaaaaaaaaalllllllllllllll llllllllllll!!!!!!!!!!!!!!!!!!!!*

Yesssssss, Julián had done it – he was the hero! In that amazing moment, his sickness seemed to fade away, while his River teammates rushed over to celebrate with him.

So, did that turn out to be Julián's big, breakthrough moment? Yes and no. After scoring that match-winning goal against Boca, Borrelli did move him into the starting line-up, but he didn't become a superstar straight away. While Julián always played well and worked hard, he was rarely River's main man, the superstar who stood out from all the rest.

That wasn't easy, and it wasn't really Julián's style either. He was a quiet, humble, unselfish guy, not a loud, arrogant show-off. The other River players loved him for that, but to take the next step and reach the first team, Julián was going to need to believe in himself a little bit more.

## CHAPTER 8

# A TURNING POINT IN TEXAS

The more time Julián spent at the River Plate academy, the more he boosted his skills and his self-belief. As he turned seventeen, however, he was still waiting for his big breakthrough, that standout moment which said, 'See, I'm a crack and I'm ready for the first team!'

Perhaps the 2017 Generation Adidas Cup could provide that moment for Julián? In April that year, River Plate travelled to Texas, USA to compete in a tournament against other Under-17 academy teams from North America, South America and Europe. How exciting! Julián couldn't wait.

'Let's go win that trophy!' he told his teammates.

It was easy to say such confident things, but could

he back it up with his performances out on the pitch? Oh yes, he could! Wearing the Number 7 shirt, Julián was River's star striker as they won all three of their group matches, against Atlanta United and the Colorado Rapids from America, and Málaga from Spain.

He scored goals himself, he set up goals for his teammates, and he never stopped running for River. What a hero!

'Keep up the great work,' Borrelli, his coach, told him, 'and soon the whole football world will know who you are.'

'Thanks, Coach – I will!'

Julián continued his fine form in the semi-finals against Independiente del Valle, a top team from Ecuador. Suddenly, with the ball at his feet, he believed he could do anything and beat anyone. In only the eighth minute, he dribbled forward into the box and set up Matías with a sublime pass through a defender's legs. *1–0!*

'Vamooooos!' Julián and Matías cheered as they celebrated the goal together.

River's young stars made a perfect partnership, and five minutes later, they swapped roles and scored again. This time, Matías flicked a long ball through to Julián, who burst past two defenders with ease and then slid a shot under the Independiente keeper. *2–0!*

*Goooooooooooooooooooaaaaaaaaaaaaaaaallllllllllllll llllllllllll!!!!!!!!!!!!!!!!!!*

Wow, Julián was on fire, and he wasn't finished yet. Early in the second half, he skipped away from his marker and raced up the right wing, before pulling the ball back for Valentín Matlis to score. *3–0!*

'Juli, you're unstoppable today!' his teammates cheered as they all piled on top of each other.

River were through to the cup final, and with a goal and two assists, Julián was their man of the match. This was it; his big, breakthrough moment, but the trophy wasn't theirs yet.

'One more game to go!' he urged his teammates on.

In the final, River faced Flamengo, one of the biggest clubs in Brazil and in the whole of South America. They were particularly famous for producing amazing attackers: Zico, Leonardo, Adriano, Gabriel

Barbosa, and most recently, Vinícius Júnior, who had just signed for Real Madrid.

Flamengo's next lot of young forwards looked pretty good too, especially Wendel and Yuri César, but River had some amazing young attackers of their own. In the eleventh minute, Matías picked out Julián with a perfect cross, and he swept the ball past the keeper. *1–0!*

*Goooooooooooooooooooooaaaaaaaaaaaaaaaaallllllllllllll llllllllllll!!!!!!!!!!!!!!!!!!!!*

'Thanks, mate!' he cheered, high-fiving Matías. It was Julián's fifth goal of the tournament and what an important one it could be!

But no, six minutes later, Yuri César equalised for Flamengo. River would have to go hunting for a winning goal again...

Early in the second half, Wendel won the ball in his own box and looked to break away on a quick counterattack, but Julián wasn't going to let that happen. He chased him all the way across the pitch and used his strength and determination to win the ball back for River.

'That's it – great battling, Juli!' Borrelli clapped and cheered on the sidelines.

Right, what next? Julián spun away from Wendel, looked up, and chipped a beautiful pass over the Flamengo defence to Sebastián Medina, who chested the ball down in the box and laid it off for the left-back, Pedro Pavlov, to score. *2–1!*

What a terrific team goal, and it had all started with Julián's hard work! He still had just enough energy to sprint over to the opposite side of the pitch and celebrate with Pedro and the others.

'We're nearly there now,' Julián told his teammates, 'but we've got to keep our concentration!'

This time, they did, and when the final whistle blew, River Plate were the winners of the 2017 Generation Adidas Cup!

'VAMOOOOOOOOOS!' Julián screamed up at the sky as he joined his teammates in a big, bouncing group hug. He felt like he had been working towards this moment for years, and at last, it had arrived. They were...

*Campeones, Campeones, Olé! Olé! Olé!*

What a night, and what a tournament! Not only had Julián helped his team to lift the trophy, but he had also stood out on his own as a superstar, winning the Golden Shoe for top goalscorer.

'Congratulations, Juli,' Borrelli said with a proud smile on his face. 'I always knew you could play like this. You've really taken your game to the next level.'

'Thanks, Coach!'

There was no stopping Julián now. He returned home to Argentina feeling more confident than ever, and his improvement was soon obvious to everyone, including one very important person: the manager of the River Plate first team.

One day, when the youth team was training with the Reserves, Marcelo Gallardo turned up to take a look at the club's future stars. After watching the session for a few minutes, he walked over to Borrelli.

'That kid over there,' Gallardo pointed across the pitch. 'What's his name?'

'Julián Álvarez.'

'Ah, so he's the kid who won us the Generation Adidas Cup! Well, he's certainly got something special.'

Borrelli nodded and smiled, 'Yes, I agree.'

Later that day, the River youth team coach got a phone call from Gallardo. 'Okay, I want to know more about Julián.'

## CHAPTER 9

# RIVER'S NEW NUMBER NINE

Hmm, interesting! Borrelli clearly believed that this Álvarez kid was a future crack, and Gallardo had heard really good things from the club scout, Gabriel Rodríguez, too. The River manager decided that it was time to test the youngster by inviting him to train with the first team.

'Yesssssssss!' Julián replied eagerly when Borrelli told him the news. Hurray, this was the moment he had been waiting for!

The night before the big day, Julián was so excited that he could hardly sleep, but the next morning when he walked into the changing room for the first time, the nerves suddenly kicked in. Woah, this was a MASSIVE

moment! Looking around, he saw players that he had
grown up cheering for as a young River fan, as well as
more recent heroes like Enzo Pérez, Nicolás De La Cruz
and Rafael Santos Borré. Now, they were about to train
*together* – unbelievable! Should Julián say something,
and if so, what and to who?

'Hey, Juli!' he heard someone call out. It was
Santiago Sosa and Cristian Ferreira, two talented
young midfielders who he knew from the year above
at the academy. 'Come sit with us in the kids' corner!'

Phew! Seeing those familiar faces did help to
settle Julián's nerves a little, but when they jogged
out onto the pitch to get warmed up, his heart was
still pounding extra fast. This was his big chance
to impress the manager; what if he did something
embarrassing, or made a really bad mistake, or just
failed to stand out?

'Come on, you can't think like that!' Julián told
himself. He had caught Gallardo's attention by playing
his own way, so he just had to keep calm and keep
doing the same things he'd always done.

*ZOOM!* During the fitness drills, Julián showed off

his speed and stamina.

*PING!* In the *rondos*, he passed the ball brilliantly under pressure.

*BANG!* When it was time to practise shooting, he hit the back of the net again and again.

Then, in the five-a-side match at the end of the session, Julián put all those talents together, and added some strength and skill.

As soon as the game kicked off, *ZOOM!* he raced around the pitch, battling to win the ball as quickly as possible. Once he had it, he turned and dribbled forward at speed, bursting past the first defender with ease. As a second closed in, *PING!* Julián slipped a clever pass through to Rafael, and then continued his run. When the ball came back to him on the edge of the box, he didn't panic, but he didn't slow down to think either. Instead, *BANG!* Julián struck his shot first time, firing the ball low and hard into the bottom corner, before the keeper could even react.

*Goooooooooooooooooooaaaaaaaaaaaaaaaalllllllllllllll llllllllllll!!!!!!!!!!!!!!!!!!*

It was a great finish, but was Gallardo watching?

Yes, he was standing there on the sidelines, with a big smile on his face.

And it turned out that Julián had impressed more than just the River manager. Ahead of the 2018 World Cup, he was invited, as one of Argentina's most promising young players, to travel to the tournament in Russia, and, best of all, to train with the senior squad.

Woah, that meant Julián was about to share a pitch with superstars like Ángel Di María, Sergio Agüero... and Messi! What on earth was he going to say to his football hero? And should he try to show off his skills in front of him? No, Julián couldn't think and act like a little fan anymore; he was seen as one of Argentina's most promising young players and he wanted to learn as much as possible from such an incredible experience. So, he tried his best to keep calm and keep doing the same things he'd always done.

*ZOOM! PING! BANG!*

*'Well played, kid!'*

Julián returned to River Plate feeling more inspired than ever. He spent the rest of the summer happily training with the first team, but as the new 2018–19 season drew near, he wondered what would happen next. Would Gallardo want him to stay with the seniors or would he send him back to the Reserves?

The early signs were good. In August, Julián was given his first official squad number to wear on the back of his shirt, and it was way better than the '29' or '37' that players from the academy usually got. Yes, Julián was River's New Number... Nine!

Wow, what a dream come true for a young striker! Over the years, so many superstars had worn the shirt for the club, including many of Julián's heroes: Alfredo Di Stéfano, Enzo Francéscoli, Radamel Falcao, and Fernando Cavenaghi. But after Marcelo Larrondo's recent return to Chile, the special number was now up for grabs.

'Thanks, Coach,' Julián beamed proudly. 'You won't regret this!'

So, did that mean he'd make his first-team debut straight away? No, sadly for the first match of the Superliga Argentina season, Julián wasn't even on the subs bench. And despite a run of three 0–0 draws in a row, by the end of September, there was still no sign of River's new Number Nine.

Oh dear, how much longer would Julián have to wait? Ages, it seemed. For now, he was the club's fifth-choice forward, behind Rafael, Lucas Pratto, Ignacio Scocco and Rodrigo Mora. 'Just be patient,' his family and coaches kept telling him, but that wasn't easy for an eager eighteen-year-old.

Luckily, by late October, the situation had changed. With River also doing really well in the Copa Libertadores, South America's biggest cup competition, Gallardo needed to rest and rotate his star players. So when Ignacio and Rafael started the semi-final against Grêmio from Brazil, it was Lucas and Rodrigo who started three days later in the Superliga Argentina against Aldosivi. And who was asked to be a substitute striker? Yes, Julián!

At last! He was so excited that he could hardly sit still next to Santiago and Cristian on the bench. Would this be the night he made his senior debut at home at the Estadio Monumental? Julián really hoped so.

It was Cristian who came on first, in the thirtieth

minute, and early in the second half, he scored an absolute worldie to give River the lead. Julián was delighted for his friend, of course, but he couldn't help thinking, 'I wish that was me out there!'

Less than ten minutes later, he got his wish. Off came Rodrigo, and on came Julián, River's New Number Nine.

'Let's do this!' he told himself as he sprinted onto the field. He only had half an hour to shine, so there was no time to waste.

Julián ran and ran, chasing after every ball. Most of his efforts came to nothing, but finally, a decent chance arrived. When Santiago collected the ball on the halfway line and looked up to play a pass, *ZOOM!* Julián was off, bursting past his marker...

'Yessssssss, Santi!'

By the time he reached the ball, Julián was already inside the Aldosivi box. What now – shoot, like the River supporters were telling him to? The angle was pretty tight, but he didn't have any teammates around to pass to, so he might as well try. Julián steadied himself and then with a powerful swing of his right leg, *BANG!* he sent the ball swerving past the goalkeeper... but unfortunately just past the goalpost too.

'Ooooh, so close!' Julián gasped, throwing his head back in disappointment. What a magical moment that would have been on his debut!

Never mind, when the final whistle blew, River were the winners and Julián was now officially a professional footballer. The crazy next chapter of his career had just begun.

One week later, Julián got the chance to play seventy minutes against Estudiantes.

Three weeks later, he came on in the semi-final of the Argentina Cup and scored in a penalty shoot-out.

Five weeks later, he was celebrating his first River assist, after setting up Rafael with a sensational pass against Gimnasia.

And six weeks later, Julián was racing onto the field in the wildest final of South America's biggest club competition.

## CHAPTER 10

# A FINAL NEVER TO FORGET

*9 December 2018, Santiago Bernabéu Stadium, Spain*

Seven years after his first trip, Julián found himself back in Madrid. But no, he wasn't about to sign for Real or Atlético; he was there as part of the River Plate squad for the second leg of the Copa Libertadores final.

So, why were they playing in Spain, instead of South America? It's a sad story . With a victory over Grêmio in the 2018 semi-finals, River had set up a final against their big Argentinian rivals, Boca Juniors. Uh-oh – the 'Superclásico' was always a fiercely passionate derby for the fans, but the two teams facing each other in the Copa Libertadores final? That had never happened before, and it turned out to be a recipe for disaster.

After a 2–2 draw in the first leg at Boca's La Bombonera Stadium, the two teams were due to play the second leg at River's Estadio Monumental on 24 November. On the way to the game, however, the Boca team bus was attacked by angry River supporters. Windows were smashed and players were hurt, which meant the match had to be rearranged. In the end, for safety reasons, the match also had to be relocated, from Argentina to Spain, from the Monumental to the Bernabéu. It was a shameful situation, but at last, two weeks later, the 2018 Copa Libertadores was about to be decided.

*Vamos, vamos, vamos, River Plate!*

*Dale, dale, dale, Boca!*

Despite moving the match to Europe, the stadium was still packed with over 60,000 supporters. One side was decorated in Boca's blue and yellow, and the other in River's red and white, but everyone roared together while the two teams walked out past the trophy and onto the pitch.

So, was Julián one of River's lucky eleven? No, sadly not. He had been a sub for the first leg, and he was a sub for the second leg too. He was really hoping that he might get to play at least a few minutes this time, though...

In the first half, Boca were the better team, and just before the break, they took the lead through Darío Benedetto.

Nooooooooo! As he watched from the bench, Julián's main emotion was disappointment, but a tiny bit of him did think, 'Maybe this means I'll get to come on...'

That didn't happen at half-time, though, and it didn't happen after sixty minutes either. Gallardo only made one change in midfield: Juan Fernando Quintero on for their captain, Leonardo.

'Come on, come on,' Julián muttered to himself as the minutes passed by, but finally, River got the goal they needed. Nacho Fernández played a lovely one-two with Exequiel Palacios and then pulled the back for Lucas to score. *1–1!*

Yessssssssssss! What a relief, River were level again,

but they still needed to find a winner...

As the match went into extra time, both teams were looking equally exhausted, but suddenly everything changed when Wilmar Barrios was sent off for Boca.

A-ha, an advantage! What River really needed now was an energetic young forward who could come on and race around the pitch, putting lots of pressure on Boca's ten tired men. That's why when Gallardo took off Exequiel in the ninety-seventh minute, he brought on Julián, rather than Rodrigo.

'Thanks, Coach!' Julián shouted, as he sprinted into position. Right, where was the ball and how could he get it?

'Yessssss!' he called out to Pity Martínez on the left wing. When the cross came in, Julián decided to hit it first time with his weaker left foot to try and catch out the keeper. He struck it beautifully, but the ball flew just wide of the top corner he was aiming for.

'Oooooh, nearly!' Julián said to himself. He was making a difference already, and hopefully, he would get at least one more chance to be the hero.

River were definitely now the team on top, but

could they grab a winning goal before the final went to penalties? They would have to be patient, and not panic. On the edge of the Boca box, Juan Fernando flicked the ball through to Julián, who spread it wide to right-back Camilo Mayada. He laid it back to Juan Fernando, who fired an unstoppable shot into the top corner. *2–1!*

'Vamoooooooooos!' Julián screamed as he threw his arms out wide and chased after Juan, the River hero.

So, was that game over and Copa Libertadores won? No, not yet; they still had some defending to do first.

Pity headed away a Boca corner kick,

Then Camilo kicked the rebound clear,

Then Julián bravely slid across the grass to try and block Fernando Gago's long-range shot. He could only get a little flick on the ball, but it was enough to slow it down and give Franco Armani a much easier save to make.

*Thanks, Juli!*

'Nearly there now, guys!' Gallardo shouted to his team from the touchline.

Five minutes – that was all Boca had left to grab

another goal. But if, on the other hand, River could score again, it really would be game over...

As Julián raced in, to challenge for the ball, the defender slipped, leaving him all on his own on the edge of the Boca box. Here it was: another chance to be the hero.

'Shooooooooot!' the River fans urged, and so that's what Julián did. *BANG!* He put plenty of power on his strike, but unfortunately, the ball flew straight into the keeper's gloves, rather than the top corner.

'Argghhhh, nooooooo!' Julián groaned with his head in his hands. What a golden opportunity to finish the game off, and he had wasted it. Oh well, it wasn't the time to worry about his mistake; they still had a few mad minutes of the final left to play.

First, Leonardo Jara's deflected shot hit the River post, and then from the Boca corner kick, Franco punched the ball out to Juan Fernando, who flicked it on for Pity to race all the way through and score. *3–1!*

'YESSSSSSSSSSSS!' Julián yelled, racing over to join the player pile-on by the corner flag. Now, it really was game over and River were the winners of the 2018

Copa Libertadores! Although eighteen-year-old Julián hadn't played many minutes in the competition, he had still played his part, and so he celebrated just like everyone else. He wandered around the pitch in a delighted daze, smiling, clapping, hugging, high-fiving, singing and dancing.

*Dale campeón, dale campeón…*

Up on the stage with his winner's medal around his neck, Julián waited patiently for his turn with the giant silver trophy. When it came, he kissed it and raised it high into the air. What a feeling! It was an amazing moment for the eighteen-year-old, and hopefully, the first of many.

## CHAPTER 11

# RIVER'S RISING STAR

So, now that he'd lifted the Copa Libertadores, what
next for River's rising star? More game-time, and some
goals, hopefully! That was Julián's aim as the Superliga
season continued, but soon he was off to Chile to
compete for his country in the Under-20 South
American Championships.

Hurray, a first call-up to the national squad! Julián
was really proud of the rapid progress he was making.
Now, he was ready to fire Argentina to glory against
the rest of South America.

'Back in 2005, Messi scored five goals in this
competition,' Julián told his River teammate Santiago,
who was in the squad too. 'That's going to be me

this year!'

It didn't quite turn out that way, though. After a slow start in the group stage, Argentina eventually got two 1–0 wins to make it through to the second round. But for Julián, despite all his tireless running, it was four games, zero goals and zero assists.

'Don't worry – keep going and they'll come,' the coach, Fernando Batista, assured him, but Julián feared that if he didn't score soon, he would lose his starting spot.

When Argentina lost 2–1 to Ecuador in their next match, Julián felt sure he'd be dropped to the bench, but no, Batista stuck with him for the game against Colombia. And in the forty-second minute, Julián stepped up to take a free kick and curled a stunning shot straight into the top corner. *1–0!*

*Goooooooooooooooooooooaaaaaaaaaaaaaaaalllllllllllllll llllllllllll!!!!!!!!!!!!!!!!!!!!*

At last, he was off the mark for Argentina!

'Yessss, Juli, I knew you could do it!' Santiago cheered as the whole team celebrated together.

That winning goal gave Julián lots of confidence

and he finished the tournament in great form.
Against Uruguay, he dropped deep to play a one-two
with Gonzalo Maroni and then poked a pass across
to Aníbal Moreno, who scored with a long-range
rocket. *1–0!*

Like Julián, Argentina seemed to be improving with
every game, but after losing to their big rivals Brazil in
the last match, they finished second behind Ecuador.
Oh well, at least they had secured a place at the 2019
Under-20 World Cup, and when it came to choosing
the Best Team of the Tournament, two of their players
were in it: Santiago… and Julián! Yes, he was really
making a name for himself, in Argentina and beyond.

So, as he returned to River, could Julián carry on
his rapid rise? Not straight away, no. For the first
few weeks, he wasn't even on the subs bench. What
was going on? Had he done something wrong? No,
not at all; Gallardo was just protecting his young
star and giving him a rest after the South American
Championships.

At last, over a month after his return, Julián was
back in the River matchday squad for the game against

Independiente. With the score stuck at 0–0, Gallardo brought him on in the fifty-seventh minute, and within seconds, he had scored his first senior goal.

As Matías Suárez chested the ball down in the centre of the field, *ZOOM!* Julián was off, sprinting in between the two centre-backs while calling for the ball. 'Yessssss!'

When Matías's pass bounced down in the box, it looked like a defender would clear it away, but no, Julián wasn't giving up and he used his strength to get there first. Then, after one touch to control the ball, he skilfully swivelled his body round and fired a powerful shot past the keeper. *1–0!*

*Goooooooooooooooooooooaaaaaaaaaaaaaaaalllllllllllllll llllllllllll!!!!!!!!!!!!!!!!!!!!*

Hurray, Julián was finally off the mark for River too! While the fans clapped and cheered in the stadium all around him, he threw his arms out wide and raced over to share the special moment with Matías.

A few weeks later, the 2018–19 Superliga season came to an end, with River finishing in fourth place. As always, they had been aiming for top spot, but never mind – they moved straight onto the next challenge: defending their Copa Libertadores trophy.

Julián only got to play five minutes in River's first five group matches, but when Matías suffered an injury, Gallardo moved him into the starting line-up for the game against Brazilian club Internacional.

'This is my chance to shine,' Julián told himself. He was determined to take it.

Right from kick-off, he raced forward to put Internacional under pressure and bravely blocked the long ball out of defence. It was going to be a good night; Julián could tell that already. In the twenty-eighth minute, he had a header cleared off the goal-line, but the Brazilians couldn't keep him out for long. Six minutes later, he timed his run to perfection to beat the offside trap, and then lobbed the ball over the Internacional keeper's head. *1–0!*

*Gooooooooooooooooooooaaaaaaaaaaaaaaaalllllllllllllll llllllllllll!!!!!!!!!!!!!!!!!!!*

What a cool, calm, striker's finish! Turning and running towards the corner flag, Julián threw his arms out in front and pretended to shoot webs from his

wrists like Spider-Man. He was having so much fun –
and it was his nickname, after all.

Unfortunately, the good times didn't last long.
Internacional equalised just before half-time, and in
the sixtieth minute, they scored again to take the lead.
Uh-oh, a defeat would be disastrous for River. Could
someone save the day?

Deep in injury time, Julián got the ball on the left
and curled one last dangerous cross into the box.
It flew just over Nacho's head, bounced and then
skipped up off the grass, forcing the Internacional
keeper to make a save. He couldn't hold onto the ball,
though, and Lucas was right there to poke home the
rebound. *2–2!*

'Yesssssss!' Julián screamed, punching the air with
both fists. He had successfully taken his chance to
shine – with a goal and an assist, he had rescued his
team from defeat.

It was the perfect way for Julián to say, 'See
you again soon!' to the River supporters, and he
set off for Europe to represent his country at the
Under-20 World Cup.

## CHAPTER 12

# JOY AND PAIN IN POLAND

For a young footballer, things didn't get any bigger or better than playing at the Under-20 World Cup. Over the years, so many superstars had emerged from the tournament:

Federico Valverde in 2017,

Paul Pogba in 2013,

Agüero in 2007,

Messi in 2005,

Saviola in 2001,

And Maradona back in 1979.

Could Julián become Argentina's next Under-20 World Cup hero? That was the aim, although he wouldn't be doing it alone. When the players set off for Poland, where the tournament was taking place, their squad looked even stronger than it had at the South American Championships.

In midfield, Santiago now had his River teammate Cristian alongside him, as well as passmaster Fausto Vera.

In attack, Argentina now had Esequiel Barco on the left wing, Pedro de la Vega on the right – and who was their star striker in the centre? Still Julián, of course!

That's how the team lined up for their first group match against South Africa, and together they got off to the perfect start. In only the fourth minute, Cristian curled a corner into the box and up jumped Fausto to head the ball in. *1–0 already!*

So, would that goal be the first of many? No, not straight away. In fact, it was South Africa who scored next, but in the second half, Argentina really showed their quality.

First, a defender fouled Cristian as he burst into the box. Penalty! Up stepped Esequiel to smash home from the spot. *2–1!*

Then after a quiet first seventy minutes, Julián

suddenly came to life. Dropping deep into midfield, he got the ball and chipped a beautiful pass through to Esequiel, who volleyed it first time into the top corner. *3–1!*

What a goal! Julián was pleased with his assist, but what he really wanted was to get on the scoresheet too. So as super sub Adolfo Gaich dribbled up the left wing a few minutes later, Julián sprinted into the six-yard box, calling for the cross. And when it arrived, he calmly guided the ball into the net. *4–1!*

*Gooooooooooooooooooooaaaaaaaaaaaaaaaaalllllllllllllll llllllllllll!!!!!!!!!!!!!!!!!!!*

Hurray, a World Cup goal to go with his assist! With a wide smile on his face, Julián ran straight over to give Adolfo a big hug. 'Thanks, mate!' he shouted up to his very tall teammate.

Argentina had the impressive opening win that they were hoping for, but Julián and his teammates knew that there would be tougher challenges ahead, starting with Portugal. They were the Under-19 European Champions, and what a fantastic front three they had: Jota, Francisco Trincão, and Rafael Leão.

It wasn't going to be easy to keep them quiet, but Argentina were determined to do it. Plus, they had a fantastic front three of their own. This time, Pedro dropped to the bench, Adolfo came in to play as the central striker, and Julián moved over to the right wing. A different position? No problem! Julián was happy to play anywhere if it helped his team to win.

In the thirty-second minute, Adolfo flicked the ball onto Esequiel, who chipped it through for Argentina's new right winger to chase...

To start with, it looked like the Portugal left-back would easily get there first, but Julián was determined to win the race, and he did, with an extra burst of pace and power. Then, with a quick Cruyff turn, he cut inside and slid the ball across to Adolfo, who swept it in off the far post. *1–0!*

'Vamooooooooos!' Julián cheered joyfully, jumping into Adolfo's arms. Speed, strength *and* skill – he had shown it all to set up another important goal for his team.

In the second half, Portugal tried their best to fight back, but instead, it was Argentina who scored again. Was it Adolfo who got the flick on Esequiel's free kick, or was it their captain Nehuén Pérez? Who card?! They had won the match and that was all that mattered.

With two victories out of two, Argentina were already through to the knockout rounds, so the manager, Batista, decided to rest Julián for the final group game against South Korea. And what happened without him? The team went 2–0 down! Eventually, in the second half, Batista did bring Julián off the bench, but despite his best efforts, he couldn't save Argentina from defeat.

Never mind, they were still in the World Cup, and Julián was back in the starting line-up four days later for their Round of 16 match against Mali. Could he help Argentina to reach the quarter-finals for the first time since 2011?

After an even first half, it was Adolfo who scored the opening goal early in the second. With a sigh of relief, Julián rushed over to celebrate with him, but twenty minutes later, Mali were level again. As extra-time approached, Batista made a big call for Argentina:

on came Agustín Urzi, and off came… Julián.

Oh. Sure, he wasn't having one of his best games, but what if the match went all the way to penalties? Wouldn't they want their best players on the pitch to take them? The manager had already made his decision, though, and Julián's day was done. Trudging off the field, he didn't argue or get angry, but his disappointment was clear for all to see.

At first, it looked like a brilliant substitution. Early in extra-time, Agustín helped start the move that ended with Esequiel's shot deflecting into the net. *2–1!*

But again, Argentina couldn't hold on to their lead. In the last minute, Mali caught them out with a quick free kick and took the match to… PENALTIES!

Nehuén went first for Argentina and scored, but next up was substitute Tomás Chancalay and… the keeper saved it!

'Nooooooooooo!' Standing on the sidelines, Julián could only watch, groan, and wish he was still out there to help his team.

Adolfo, Santiago and Fausto all scored, but unfortunately for them, so did all five of Mali's takers.

It was all over, and Argentina were out.

Julián's Under-20 World Cup dream was over, but hopefully one day, he would get another chance to shine for his country, in the senior competition.

## CHAPTER 13

# A TALE OF TWO CUP FINALS

When Julián returned home after the Under-20 World
Cup, there was no time to feel too sorry for himself.
He had work to do at River Plate: games to play, goals
to score, and a starting spot to earn.

None of that was going to be easy, though, because
the club was well-stocked with strikers. Matías and
Rafael were both on fire, and so were super-subs
Lucas and Ignacio. For now, the most Gallardo
could give young Julián was a few appearances
off the bench:

Eleven minutes in the Superliga against Lanús,

Eight minutes in the Copa Libertadores semi-final
against Boca Juniors...

But that wasn't enough time to shine – how and when would Julián ever get a proper chance to play? All he could do was keep working hard and wait for his big moment to arrive.

Might it come before the end of 2019? Late November to early December was set to be a crucial time for River because they were competing in not one, but TWO cup finals. First up: their second Copa Libertadores final in a row, this time against Brazilian club Flamengo.

For the big match, River were travelling to Peru with a larger squad than usual: twenty-three players in total, including Julián.

Yessssss! Julián couldn't wait. While he knew that he probably wouldn't start in the final, he hoped that Gallardo might at least give him a few minutes later on, like he had the year before against Boca. And he was right about that. With River already winning 1–0 thanks to a goal from Rafael, their manager made the bold decision to take off Nacho, a natural midfielder, and replace him with Julián.

'Just do what you always do,' Gallardo told him

on the touchline. 'Run hard, put pressure on the defenders, and get us a second goal!'

'Yes, Boss!'

Julián did his very best to do what his manager asked. He ran hard, up and down the right wing, and he put the Flamengo players under lots of pressure, but unfortunately, he failed to score a second goal. In fact, he hardly touched the ball at all.

With five minutes to go, however, River were still winning 1–0, and that was all that really mattered. They just had to hold on now...

But no, in the eighty-ninth minute, they gave the ball away in midfield and Flamengo flew forward on a quick counterattack. Uh-oh – it was five of them against just four River defenders! Julián chased back as fast as he could, but he couldn't stop Bruno Henrique's pass to Giorgian de Arrascaeta, or his cross to Gabriel Barbosa at the back post. *1–1!*

'What? Nooooooo!' For a moment, Julián stood there frozen in disbelief, with his hands on his hips, on the edge of his own box. But what good would that do? His team needed him to keep going and help them win. So, forward he raced to try and become River's hero.

Unfortunately, however, Julián didn't score the next goal, and neither did any of his teammates. The matchwinner turned out to be Flamengo's Gabriel Barbosa. With seconds to go, the Brazilian striker scored again, breaking the hearts of every River player and supporter.

Julián was both of those things, and so it was the worst feeling in the world. Losing any cup final was bad, but to lose it like that, letting in two goals in the last five minutes? It was truly terrible! Although he really didn't want to, Julián did go up to collect his runners-up medal, and then stood to clap for the Flamengo players. But after that, he got off the pitch as quickly as possible. He needed to be alone for a while.

The only good news for Julián and his teammates was that River still had another cup final to play: in the Copa Argentina, against Central Córdoba. It was a chance for them to start putting things right straight away, and Julián was desperate to play his part. Growing up in Calchín, Central had been one of his local football clubs, but he loved the idea of scoring against them.

Again, Julián started on the subs bench, and again, Gallardo brought him on before the seventieth minute, with River already winning 1–0. This time, however, things turned out very differently. Two minutes after he came on, Nacho made it 2–0, and six minutes after that? It was Julián's turn to score.

As Nacho dribbled his way up the left wing, Julián waited in the middle, staying alert and onside. Then, when at last the cross arrived, he didn't panic or try to blast it with power. Instead, Julián calmly guided the ball past the keeper. *3–0!*

*Goooooooooooooooooooooaaaaaaaaaaaaaaaalllllllllllllll llllllllllll!!!!!!!!!!!!!!!!!!!!*

Yessssss, he had done it; he was a cup final hero! After a quick Spider-Man celebration, Julián ran over to thank Nacho for the assist. Soon, they were surrounded by all their River teammates, including the substitutes.

'*Great work, Juli!*'

'*Nice one, Nacho!*'

'VAMOOOOOOOS!'

'Well done, guys – we're going to win the cup!'

It was so nice to have something happy to smile about again, after the sad story of the Flamengo final. This time, when the game ended, Julián walked around the pitch with his head held high, hugging his teammates, one by one. This time, when he went up to collect his winner's medal, he couldn't wait to wear it proudly around his neck. And this time, when the trophy was lifted high into the air and fireworks filled the sky, Julián was there, at the centre of it all, dancing and singing along with his teammates:

*Dale campeón, dale campeón...*

## CHAPTER 14

# FOREVER THE HUMBLE KID FROM CALCHÍN

Back in his hometown, 400 miles from Buenos Aires, Julián had not been forgotten. No, the local people were following his progress closely, and they were so pleased to see the Little Spider of Calchín living up to all his early potential. Their golden boy was about to become River's next big crack, and no-one was prouder than his old Atlético coach, Rafael Varas.

'Scoring in the cup final, eh? I always knew that kid of yours had something special!' Varas told Julián's dad Gustavo when they bumped into each other one day, not at the football club, but outside a shop in the centre of town. While Varas loved working with Calchín's most promising young players, unfortunately that wasn't his main job. In order to earn enough money for his family, he also drove around selling food to supermarkets.

'Well, Julián definitely couldn't have done it without your help!' Gustavo replied warmly. 'We'll forever be grateful to you – I hope you know that.'

'Oh I do!' Rafael said, as the smile on his face grew even wider. 'Did Julián tell you that he sent me a signed River shirt recently? It was so kind of him to think of me, and he even wrote, "To my first coach who accompanied me for my first steps". What a beautiful message from a beautiful young man!"'

Gustavo, the proud father, nodded. 'Good, I'm glad to hear it… and how are things with you, Rafael?'

The coach shrugged and laughed. 'Oh you know me, I'm the same as always – still working hard every hour of the day, and still searching for the next young Julián to take Calchín by storm!'

After some more friendly chat about football and family, it was time for Gustavo to say goodbye and head off home. But before he left, he looked back at the Atlético coach who was still stood there, struggling

to fit all of his big food boxes back into his small car…
A-ha! Gustavo had an idea that he wanted to talk to
Julián about.

The day after that meeting in town, Rafael received
a surprise phone call. It was Gustavo:

'Rafael, are you at home?'

'Yes… why?' he answered, but Gustavo ignored
his question.

'Great, I'm coming over!' he said and then ended
the call straight away.

Why? What did Gustavo want to talk to him
about? While Rafael sat there waiting and wondering,
suddenly he heard a loud noise coming from outside.

*'BEEP, BEEP! BEEP, BEEP!'*

What on earth was going on? When Rafael went to
the window to look, he saw Gustavo sitting there in a
white van so new and clean that it sparkled in the sun.
It was a beauty, but it didn't make any sense – why
would Gustavo need a big vehicle like that? There was
only one way to find out…

'Hey, nice van!' Rafael called out from his
front doorstep.

'I'm glad you like it,' Gustavo replied with a grin. Then he got out, walked over to Rafael and handed him the keys. 'Because it's for you!'

What, really?! Rafael didn't know what to say. The Álvarez family had bought him the new van that he really needed for his business? What a generous gift! With tears streaming down his cheeks, he hugged Gustavo and thanked him again and again.

'Oh no, it's not from me,' Gustavo grinned. 'Go and take a look at the back!'

Below one of the van windows, Rafael found the only clues he needed: the word 'Gracias!' (the Spanish for 'thanks!') written in curly letters next to a picture of a spider hanging down from its web.

'Julián!' Rafael gasped, overwhelmed with the emotion of the moment. First, a signed shirt, and now a brand-new van? He really couldn't thank the youngster enough. It was clear that just as Calchín hadn't forgotten Julián, Julián also hadn't forgotten Calchín. The kid was still as humble and kind as ever.

That night, Rafael received another phone call, although this time, it wasn't such a surprise. He had an idea who it might be:

'So, do you like your new van, Coach?'

'Yes, I love it, Julián, but–'

Rafael began to sob, but his former superstar stopped him straight away.

'Hey, it's the least I could do to say thank you for everything you've done for me. Enjoy it – you earned it. Gracias and see you again soon!'

## CHAPTER 15

# LEARNING AT THE HIGHEST LEVEL

So, now that he was a River Plate cup final hero, could Julián take the next step from super sub to regular starter? That was his big task for 2020; he was determined to make it his breakthrough year.

'If I keep making the most of every chance I get,' he discussed with his brothers, 'then soon the manager will have no choice but to play me all the time!'

In February, River were 1–0 down against Defensa y Justicia when Gallardo called for Julián to come on and save the day. Hurray, he couldn't wait! Just seconds after sprinting onto the pitch, he got the ball on the left wing and dribbled dangerously into the box.

'Shooooot!' the fans urged, but no, when his path was blocked by two defenders, Julián was calm and clever enough to look up and pass the ball across to Nacho instead. Nacho then played it through to Nicolás de la Cruz, who was fouled as he tried to turn – penalty! *1–1!*

'Vamoooooooooos!' Julián roared as he celebrated the goal with his teammates. What an immediate impact!

Julián really didn't want to stay a super sub forever, though. So far, he had proved that he could race around the pitch for the last thirty minutes of a match, terrorising tired defences, but shining for the full ninety in game after game, scoring goal after goal? That top-class consistency was something that he was still working towards.

A few days later, Julián got a rare chance to start for River in the Copa Libertadores, away against L.D.U. Quito from Ecuador. Hurray, he couldn't wait! He rushed around the pitch like it was his debut appearance, but despite his best, eager efforts, he struggled to get himself on the ball and into the game. Even in the second half, when he spun brilliantly and fired a low shot towards the bottom corner, the goal he desperately wanted didn't come. Instead, the Quito keeper made an excellent save to tip it round the post.

'Ahhhhh so close!' Julián groaned, throwing his hands to his head. It just wasn't his night. Soon after that, with River losing 2–0 and down to ten men, his manager decided to take him off. With shoulders slumped, Julián made the slow, sad walk back to the subs bench. As he sat there watching the rest of the game, he kept going through the missed opportunities in his head.

'If only Cristian had passed that ball to me instead of shooting!'

'If only I had closed down their midfielder slightly quicker!'

'If only I had aimed for the other bottom corner!'

But it was too late to change any of that; all he could do was move forward and correct those mistakes for next time.

*Play, practise, improve. Play, practise, improve...*

Yes, Julián knew that he still had a lot to learn at the highest level, especially about dealing with close attention from clever defenders. As word spread across Argentina and beyond about River's next big thing, Julián became a target for the toughest centre-backs.

'Oh, you think you're a superstar, do you?' they challenged him. 'Well, let's see if you can handle a bit of pressure!'

And by 'pressure', they meant:

Pushes in the back, and pulls on the shirt,

*'Foul!'*

Nasty words in his ears, and nasty kicks on his ankles.

*'Come on, ref!'*

It was like Julián's crack days at Atlético Calchín all over again! But no matter what happened to him out on the pitch, he never lost his cool. What was the point in fighting with defenders or arguing with referees? That wasn't going to help his team to win. Instead, it was much better to keep calm and keep learning, and let his dancing feet do the talking…

Unfortunately, in March 2020, the season was suspended due to the coronavirus pandemic, but when football returned in September, Julián came back with a real bang in the Copa Libertadores. This time, there were no mistakes, and no 'If only's'.

Away against São Paulo, Julián set up River's first goal for Rafael and then reacted quickly in the box to score the second himself.

*Goooooooooooooooooooaaaaaaaaaaaaaaaaalllllllllll lllllllllllllllll!!!!!!!!!!!!!!!!!!!*

Julián threw his arms out wide and raced over to the corner flag to celebrate in front of the fans. It felt so great to finally be on the scoresheet for his team again!

And after that, the goals kept coming:

First a powerful, right-foot blast against Deportivo Binacional,

Then two more to beat São Paulo at home!

Next up: the return game against L.D.U. Quito. In the away match back in March, Julián had really struggled to get into the game, but two major things had changed since then:

Julián had become a regular starter for River, and he had found his best scoring form.

So as Rafael received the ball in the middle of the field, *ZOOM!* Julián was off, bursting in between two defenders and calling for the pass. When it arrived, he knew exactly what he was about to do. He took one touch to control the ball and then *CHIP!* he dinked it over the diving keeper and into the net.

*Goooooooooooooooooooaaaaaaaaaaaaaaaaalllllllllll llllllllllllllll!!!!!!!!!!!!!!!!!!!!*

What a cool and confident finish – Julián was on fire! He had now scored in his last four Copa Libertadores games in a row.

As he picked himself up off the grass and ran over to Rafael, the smile on Julián's face was clear for all to see. He was really enjoying himself at the highest level now. He was showing everyone that of course he could shine for the full ninety minutes in game after game, scoring goal after goal! It had taken a lot of learning, patience and practice to get there, but Julián's big breakthrough had just begun.

## CHAPTER 16

# THE BIG BREAKTHROUGH

By the end of 2020, people were already calling Julián 'the new Agüero', and he was being linked with some of Europe's top clubs:

An Italian adventure at Juventus, alongside fellow Argentinian forward Paulo Dybala?

Or maybe a move to Atlético Madrid, to work under Argentinian manager Diego Simeone?

Julián was honoured to hear the rumours, but no, he didn't feel ready to leave River Plate just yet. He still had work to do: more improvements to make, more goals to score, and more trophies to win, starting with the Supercopa Argentina.

For the big final against Racing, Julián was only

named as a substitute, but boy did he make an impact when he came on. In his second minute on the pitch, he got the ball near the halfway line and dribbled all the way into the box. Then, when he got there, he calmly cut inside and whipped a powerful shot past the keeper.

*Goooooooooooooooooooaaaaaaaaaaaaaaaaallllllllllllll llllllllllll!!!!!!!!!!!!!!!!!!!*

What a run, and what a finish! Jumping into his teammates' arms, Julián was bursting with pride and joy. He always loved scoring, but scoring big goals in big games? There was no better feeling in the world!

With the Supercopa won, Julián's big breakthrough continued. In June 2021, he was called up to the senior national team for the first time and, when he ran on to replace Ángel Di María in the game against Chile, two of his childhood dreams came true at once.

Hurray, he was playing for Argentina... and with Messi!

Racing around the pitch, Julián was as professional as ever, but once the game – his international debut – was over, he was able to stop and ask himself, 'Did that *really* just happen?'

'Yes!' was the answer and there was more madness
to come. A week later, when the Argentina manager
Lionel Scaloni announced his twenty-eight-man squad
for the Copa América, there was his name under the
list of forwards:

Lionel Messi, Lautaro Martínez, Joaquin Correa,
Sergio Agüero... and Julián Álvarez.

Woah, really?! It was another unbelievable moment
in an unbelievable month for the kid from Calchín.

With so many superstars to choose from, Julián
knew that he probably wouldn't get to play in the
tournament, but just being a part of the squad, and
learning from Messi and Agüero, was the chance of
a lifetime.

As it turned out, Julián did get to play some minutes
– thirty-seven of them, in fact. With Argentina
already winning 3–0 in their final group game against
Bolivia, Scaloni decided to bring on his youngest star.
Hurray, this was it: Julián's chance to shine at the
Copa América!

Sadly, he didn't manage to score himself, but he did

play a part in the passing move that led to Argentina's fourth goal. So while Lionel and Lautaro stood there celebrating together, they welcomed Julián into their huddle. Woah, was he really sharing a hug with Messi, his football hero? It still felt too good to be true!

For the rest of the tournament, right through to the final, Julián supported his team from the sidelines. But when they beat Brazil to win the Copa América trophy for the first time in twenty-eight years, Julián rushed out onto the pitch with the rest of the squad, bouncing up and down with delight.

*Vamos, vamos Argentina!*

*Dale campeón, dale campeón...*

What an unforgettable experience! Julián returned to River feeling more determined than ever. He didn't want to be the kid they called 'The Little Spider' anymore; he was twenty-one years old now and he was ready to reach the next level. Yes, his big breakthrough had already begun, but now it was time for part two: becoming a crack.

Because if Julián wanted to become Messi's partner up front for the national team, Julián needed to start

scoring goal after goal in game after game, in the
Copa Libertadores but also the Superliga Argentina. A
superstar striker – that's what he wanted to be, and
that's what River needed him to be. Rafael, Lucas and
Ignacio had all left the club, so who was going to score
the goals now?

'ME!' Julián declared, and he kicked off
with a masterclass against Messi's old club,
Newell's Old Boys.

*ZOOM!* He skipped away from two defenders and
set up Nicolás to score the first goal. *1–0!*

*BANG!* He fired in River's second with his weaker
left foot. *2–1!*

*PING!* He played a lovely one-two with Jorge
Carrascal. *3–1!*

*BANG!* He scored again, this time with his
right foot. *4–1!*

Two goals and two assists – what a wonderful
performance! But could Julián keep it up? Oh
yes, he could.

In the next game, he flicked in the winner against
Arsenal Sarandí. *GOAL!*

Six days later, he chased back to steal the ball off the Central Córdoba centre-back and then slid a great pass through to Jorge. *ASSIST!*

Then in the second half, he raced in to reach the ball first and blasted an unstoppable shot from the edge of the box. *GOAL!*

'VAMOOOOOOOOOS!' Julián roared as he jumped up and punched the air. That made it four goals and three assists in his last three league games. Those were the stats of a true superstar striker! He was in the best form of his life and up next was River's biggest game of the season: the Superclásico against Boca.

When the two teams walked out at the Estadio Monumental, the pressure was really on Julián. He wasn't a super sub anymore; he was River's star player and top scorer, and so the fans were expecting him to do something special.

No problem! In the twenty-fifth minute, Julián won the ball in the middle of the field, skipped away from one tackle, and then dribbled forward. A Boca midfielder chased him all the way, but with a clever body swerve, Julián cut inside and created enough space for the shot. *BANG!* From thirty yards out, he sent the ball curling and dipping over the keeper and into the top corner. *1–0!*

*Goooooooooooooooooooooaaaaaaaaaaaaaaaaalllllllllllllll llllllllllllll!!!!!!!!!!!!!!!!!!!!!*

Woah, what a sensational strike! As he turned and raced away to celebrate with the fans, Julián felt on top of the world, as if he could do absolutely anything on the football pitch. Score a second goal? Sure! When Santiago Simón fired a low cross into the six-yard box just before half-time, Julián was there to calmly sweep the ball into the bottom corner. *2–0!*

*Goooooooooooooooooooooaaaaaaaaaaaaaaaaalllllllllllllll llllllllllllll!!!!!!!!!!!!!!!!!!!!!*

From long-range rockets to close-range tap-ins – Julián was showing that he was a superstar striker who could score in so many different ways. What a helpful hero to have! The River players threw their arms around him and the supporters chanted his name.

*Álvarez! Álvarez! Álvarez!*

What a feeling, and what a night! There was no stopping Julián now. How did he follow up those two game-winning goals against Boca? By scoring a hat-trick two weeks later against San Lorenzo!

## CHAPTER 17

# CHAMPIONS OF ARGENTINA!

Hat-trick hero Julián had scored ten goals for the 2021 season already, and there were still nine games to go. Could he finish as the league's highest scorer? His team River Plate, meanwhile, were four points clear at the top of the table. Could they hold on and lift their first title for seven years?

A lot could change in the last weeks of the season, but the River squad was united and they had the perfect blend of youth and experience. On the one hand, there was the golden generation coming through from the club's academy:

Defender Felipe Peña Biafore,

Midfielder Enzo Fernández,

Forwards Santiago Simón, Benjamín Rollheiser, and of course the best of them all, Julián!

That was a lot of energy and exciting talent to have in one team, but luckily they also had wise heads like captain and goalkeeper Franco Armani, plus midfielders Enzo Pérez and Leonardo Ponzio, to keep things calm and organised.

'Keep going, we can't let this slip!' Franco clapped and cheered from his goal.

At the other end of the pitch, Julián was just as determined to help lead his team to the title. One game at a time, one win at a time…

*Talleres de Cordóba 0 River Plate 2,*

Julián set up the second goal with a bursting run and pass.

*River Plate 3 Argentinos Juniors 0,*

Braian Romero assisted Julián, and then Julián assisted Braian. What terrific teamwork!

*Estudiantes 1 River Plate 1,*

It wasn't the win that Julián wanted, but at least it was another point to add to the total. They were up to forty-three points now, seven ahead of Talleres in second place, with only six games to go. Next up: Patronato…

Midfielder Agustín Palavecino scored River's first goal of the match, but after that, it turned into the Julián Álvarez Show.

When the Patronato keeper spilled the ball in the six-yard box, Julián was there to pounce. *2–0!*

Eight minutes later, when the keeper took too long to clear the ball, Julián rushed in to tackle him, before tapping into an empty net from a really tight angle. *3–0!*

That was probably game won for River, but Julián didn't see it that way. As a superstar striker, he always wanted more. So, when Agustín's shot was saved, he was the first to react and head home the rebound. *4–0!*

'Man, that keeper must really hate you,' his teammates joked with him. 'Did you see the way he threw his water bottle – I'd watch out if I was you!'

But no, Julián wasn't afraid of anything. He was delighted to score his second hat-trick of the season, but why stop there? It wasn't even half-time yet!

Although it took a while to come, he did finally add a fourth goal. Bursting into the box to reach Jorge's pass, he calmly chipped the ball over the outrushing keeper. *5–0!*

*Goooooooooooooooooooaaaaaaaaaaaaaaaallllllllllllll llllllllllll!!!!!!!!!!!!!!!!!!!!*

His fifteenth goal of the season! Wasn't Julián starting to get bored of scoring so many? No way, he celebrated every goal like it was his first because it was the greatest feeling in the world! And more importantly, his goals were leading his team towards the league title, one game at a time...

*Platense 0 River Plate 1,*

It was Julián who started the match-winning move, wide on the right wing, and it was Julián who finished it off too, racing into the box to beat the keeper to Enzo's clever lobbed pass.

*Goooooooooooooooooooaaaaaaaaaaaaaaaallllllllllllll llllllllllll!!!!!!!!!!!!!!!!!!!!*

'Yessssssssssss!' River's brightest young stars cheered as they celebrated the goal together. For Julián, it was goal number sixteen of the season, and certainly one of the most important. They were so close now, just one win away from the trophy...

The Monumental Stadium was packed with 65,000 fans for River's next match against Racing. Would this be the day their team won the league title again?

For the first twenty-five minutes, the game was tense and even, but eventually, River got the breakthrough they needed. Enzo dribbled up the left wing and slipped a pass through to Agustín, who slid the ball through the keeper's legs. *1–0!*

'Vamoooooooooooos!' Julián yelled out with a mix of joy and relief as he raced across the pitch to celebrate with his teammates. They were so nearly there now!

The goal really settled the nerves of the River players, and after that, they cruised to a comfortable victory.

Agustín's pass flicked off a defender's leg and rolled towards Julián, who fired a low shot into the bottom corner. *2–0!*

Then midway through the second half, Braian beat the keeper to finish off a brilliant team move. *3–0!*

And finally, with fifteen minutes to go, Braian scored again, after some high-energy pressing from

River's attackers. *4–0!*

Soon, it was all over, and they had done it, with three games to spare. River Plate were the Champions of Argentina again!

The players sang and danced around the pitch, while fireworks exploded in the night sky above them. And that was just the beginning. When Franco and Leonardo lifted the trophy together, there was silver confetti too, plus pounding drums, and lots more singing and dancing:

*Dale campeón, dale campeón!*

From the stadium, the party then spread out into the streets and squares of Buenos Aires. The city was painted red and white.

*Vamos, vamos, vamos, River Plate!*

Unbelievable! It was a night and a feeling that Julián would never, ever forget. He had won major trophies with River before – the Copa Libertadores in 2018 and then the Copa Argentina in 2019 – but back then he'd been a young super sub. This trophy felt different because he had played a massive part in winning it, playing almost every minute of every match, and scoring again and again as River's superstar striker. So Julián was determined to enjoy every moment; he had earned it.

'¡Dale Campeón!' he posted for his fans on social media the next day, alongside funny photos of him holding the trophy while wearing a top hat and then a Spider-Man mask.

And Julián's amazing season wasn't over yet. He grabbed his eighteenth goal in River's last game against Atlético Tucumán to win an individual award to go with the team trophy: the Golden Boot, for being the league's top scorer.

## CHAPTER 18

# BIG NEWS FOR THE BIRTHDAY BOY

As soon as River's title celebrations were over, talk turned to the next challenge. How long would the club be able to keep hold of their top young talents? Enzo and Santiago were both already being linked with moves to Europe, while Julián, their superstar striker, was wanted by all of the biggest football clubs:

Manchester United,

Manchester City,

Bayern Munich,

Inter Milan,

Barcelona,

Real Madrid...

Yes, Julián was now seen as one of the best young players in not just South America, but the whole wide world! So, was he ready to take the next step and leave Argentina, and if so, where did he want to go?

At first, it looked like Manchester United were leading the way, but really, there were two other clubs that Julián loved more.

'On the Playstation, I play with Barcelona or Manchester City,' he had told a journalist the previous year. Barcelona because of Messi, and Manchester City because of Agüero.

Barcelona, however, were now a club in crisis. They were more than £1 billion in debt, plus Messi had recently signed for PSG. So no, Barca didn't feel like a good fit for Julián, even if they could afford to buy him.

Okay – what about moving to Manchester City instead to become 'the next Agüero'? As a kid, growing up in Calchín, Julián still remembered watching the striker's 2012 title-winning goal. What a hero! Agüero had just left the club after ten

amazing years, but he thought that Julián signing for
City was a great idea.

'Trust me, you'll love it there and you'll win lots
of trophies!' Agüero told Julián enthusiastically.
'And if you don't believe me, talk to Pep – he'll
persuade you!'

'Pep' was Pep Guardiola, the most famous football
manager on the planet, who had links to both of
Julián's favourite clubs and both of his favourite
players. At Barcelona, he had helped turn Messi into
the best player in the world, and at Manchester City,
he had won the Premier League title three times
with Agüero as his main goalscorer.

The chance to work with Pep and become his
next Argentinian ace? Yes please! Julián loved the
sound of that.

And Pep loved the sound of working with him too.
City's South America scout, Joan Patsy, had been
watching Julián since he was sixteen years old, and
he was a huge fan of his many talents.

'He's quick, aggressive, strong and skilful,' Patsy
told Guardiola. 'He loves scoring goals and he loves

setting them up too. Plus, he can play anywhere across the forward line: right wing, left wing, Number 9 or second striker.'

Yes, Julián was perfect for City's fluid style of play! For a while, however, the club had kept watching and waiting, until in January 2022, they couldn't wait any longer. It was time to act, before another team beat them to him.

'Julián, I can see that you're already a really great player,' Pep explained when they finally met each other, 'but we've got big plans to take you to the next level.'

Wow, that sounded super exciting! Julián was impressed by everything he saw and heard at City: the ambition, the organisation, the facilities, the coaches, and of course, the other players. Kevin De Bruyne, Bernardo Silva, Raheem Sterling, Phil Foden – it would be a dream come true to call them teammates and chase all the top European trophies together.

So at the age of twenty-two, Julián decided that he was ready to leave River Plate and Argentina behind and set off on a new Premier League adventure. Now, it was just up to the two clubs to agree a transfer fee...

The big news was finally announced on 31 January, Julián's birthday, and it was the perfect present. For a bargain price of £14 million, he had been signed by Manchester City!

'Julián is a player we have monitored for some time,' said Txiki Begiristain, the club's Director of Football. 'I really believe we can provide him with the right conditions to fulfil his potential and become a top player.'

'Yes please!' Julián thought to himself. He couldn't wait to take his game to the next level.

Julián wasn't moving to Manchester straight away, though. City knew how hard it could be for young players to adapt to life in a new country with a new language, and so they didn't want to put too much pressure on their new South American star. There was no rush; all the packing and planning, the sad goodbyes and nervous hellos, could wait a little longer. For now, Julián was returning home to River Plate for six more months, on loan for the rest of the season.

## CHAPTER 19

# SAYING GOODBYE IN STYLE

Six more months at River Plate – right, what could Julián achieve in that time? Although he would soon be joining Manchester City, he was determined to say goodbye in style, by scoring as many goals as possible for his favourite team.

In February 2022, Julián fired his way to another hat-trick against Patronato in the Copa Argentina...

...And then in May, he grabbed a DOUBLE hat-trick against Alianza Lima in the Copa Libertadores.

Yes, that's right, he scored six goals in one game!

*ZOOM!* Julián burst into the box and guided the ball past the keeper.

*WHIZZ!* He slid into the six-yard box to reach

Santiago's low cross.

*BANG!* From thirty yards out, he sent a shot dipping and swerving into the bottom corner.

*Goooooooooooooooooooooaaaaaaaaaaaaaaaaallllllllllllll llllllllllll!!!!!!!!!!!!!!!!!!!!*

Hurray, one hat-trick completed, and it wasn't even half-time yet! But Julián didn't slow down in the second half; no matter what the score was, he always gave everything out on the football pitch.

*ZOOM!* He raced in to close down the keeper and then passed the ball into an empty net.

*DINK!* One-on-one with the keeper, Julián stayed calm and scored with a cheeky chip.

*OLÉ!* With the ball at his feet, he weaved his way through the box, past one defender and then another, before smashing a left-foot shot into the bottom corner.

*Goooooooooooooooooooooaaaaaaaaaaaaaaaaallllllllllllll llllllllllll!!!!!!!!!!!!!!!!!!!!*

Sensational – a second hat-trick completed, and with ten minutes to spare!

'Vamooooooos!' Julián roared with passion as he

leapt up and punched the air. He was in unstoppable form, making everything look so easy, especially scoring goals.

'Well done, Juli!' his River teammates congratulated him. 'But what are we going to do without you?!'

And the supporters celebrating in the stadium were wondering the exact same thing. Who would be their new hero, and where would all the goals come from? One thing was for sure: River were really going to miss their superstar striker when he finally waved goodbye.

Meanwhile, 11,000 miles away in Manchester, word quickly spread about Julián's amazing double hat-trick.

*Have you seen all the goals? Álvarez looks like the real deal, doesn't he!*

*Yeah, and for £14 million – what a bargain!*

*Him up front with Haaland? Now that's a strikeforce I'd love to see!*

Yes – just days before Julián's double hat-trick, City had confirmed a deal for another young striker for next season: Borussia Dortmund's destroyer, Erling Haaland, for a fee of over £50 million.

It was a massive signing for the club and Erling was sure to go straight into the starting line-up. So, was Julián worried? Not at all; he was even more excited about his move to Manchester City! He would happily play in whichever position Pep wanted him to: right wing, left wing, or, even better, as a second striker alongside Erling.

Erling's speed, strength and shooting, combined with Julián's energy, skill and creativity – it sounded like the perfect partnership!

It wasn't time for Julián to focus on his City future just yet, though. He still had one more month of matches to play for River Plate...

To everyone's surprise, Julián failed to score at all in his first two games of the new Argentine league season, but in game number three against Unión, he was at the centre of everything.

Julián set up Braian with a beautiful through-ball. *ASSIST!*

From the edge of the box, he looked up and chipped a perfect pass through to Enzo. *ASSIST!*

*Thanks, Juli!*

He was always happy to help his teammates, but now he wanted to score some goals of his own. Racing onto a loose ball, Julián faked to shoot high but went low instead, leaving the keeper totally fooled.

*Goooooooooooooooooooooaaaaaaaaaaaaaaaaallllllllllllllll llllllllllll!!!!!!!!!!!!!!!!!!!!!*

And in the very last minute, he beat the keeper again. *GOAL!*

But with each game and each goal, Julián's time at River was running out. After one more strike against Huracán in the league, he stepped out at the Monumental Stadium to play his last game for the club in the Copa Libertadores against Vélez Sarsfield. With his family there watching in the crowd, it was a very emotional night for Julián, but it turned out to be a very frustrating one too.

In the first few minutes, Braian broke through and poked a shot just wide of the post. *Nearly!*

Then early in the second half, so did Nicolás. *So close!*

With fifteen minutes to go, Matías finally scored with a diving header, but no, the goal was disallowed because of a handball. *So unlucky!*

And Julián? As always, River's superstar striker kept running and running, but for once, he was struggling to get on the ball and into the game. Every cross seemed to fly just over his head, every pass seemed just too far for him to reach, and whenever he got past one defender, he was surrounded by two or three more!

The match wasn't over yet, though. In the last seconds, Julián raced across the pitch to try and win one last throw-in for his team, but the referee awarded a free kick to Velez instead.

'Noooo!' he yelled, throwing the ball away in anger, and getting a yellow card for it.

Julián had been so desperate to say goodbye in style with a game-winning goal, but sadly, it wasn't to be. The match finished in a 0–0 draw.

Oh well, it wasn't the River ending that he'd hoped for, but there was no time to worry about that. The very next day, he was off, on his way to Manchester City.

'Welcome Álvarez,' the club announced to the world. 'Our new Number 19.'

But while Julián was super excited about his future at City, he was never going to forget his past, and his incredible rise at River Plate. He would always be so grateful for everything that his old club had done for him.

'Ever since I first arrived in 2016, you have always looked after me, protected me, made me feel comfortable, and helped me to grow, as a player but also as a person,' Julián thanked everyone in a video message on social media. 'I am really proud of what I achieved as a twenty-two-year-old at this club, and I leave with so many great memories and great friends. I want you all to know that I will always be a River fan.'

## CHAPTER 20

# EARLY DAYS WITH ERLING

So, how would Julián settle into his new life at
Manchester City?

Away from football, there were many things that
he'd need to get used to, like the tricky English
language and the rainy English weather.

And even at City, Julián had lots of adapting to do.
Suddenly, for the first time in his football career, every
aspect of his life was looked after. The club had people
to plan, and technology to check:

What he ate,

What he drank,

What workouts he did in the gym,

And even what time he went to bed and woke up!

'Shhhhh, they're probably listening to us right now!'
Julián joked with his brothers, Rafael and Agustin,
who had moved to Manchester with him.

Agüero had warned him about the high standards
Pep expected from his players, but it was still a bit
of a shock. Julián was desperate to impress his new
manager, though, and the club's preseason tour to the
USA was the perfect place to start.

In their first match against Club América, Julián
got the chance to play as City's main striker, and he
certainly made the most of it. Although he didn't
score himself, he worked really hard for his new team,
pressing aggressively from the front. Afterwards, Pep
was full of praise.

'Julián was incredible,' he said. 'We are delighted.'

Phew! So far, so good, but it was only one friendly.
How would Julián perform once the proper, competitive
matches began?

First up: Liverpool, in the FA Community Shield.
For the big game, City started with a front three of
Jack Grealish on the left, Riyad Mahrez on the right,
and Erling in the middle, but with his team 1–0

down after sixty minutes, Pep decided to make a double change:

Phil Foden on for Jack,

And Julián on for Riyad.

What an opportunity to impress, and also what an opportunity to win a trophy on his debut! Full of determination, Julián raced straight into the action.

'Yesssss!' he called out, making a sudden run from the right wing to the centre.

When Bernardo's pass arrived, Julián headed the ball back to Erling, and then carried on running into the box, just in case...

Erling passed to Kevin, who crossed it to Phil as he sprinted in at the back post. Phil's first shot was saved, and so was his second, but who was there to poke home at the third attempt? Yes, Julián!

*Gooooooooooooooooooooaaaaaaaaaaaaaaaaalllllllllllllll llllllllllll!!!!!!!!!!!!!!!!!!!!*

Just as Julián turned away to celebrate, he spotted that the linesman's flag was up for offside. 'Nooooooooo!' he groaned, throwing his hands to his head. But after a long VAR check...the goal was given!

'Yesssssssssss!' Julián cried out, pumping his fists at the crowd. It certainly wasn't one of the best goals he'd ever scored, but who cared about that? Not him!

Unfortunately, Liverpool went on to win the match 3–1, but it wasn't all bad news. At least Julián was off the mark already: one game, one goal.

When the Premier League season kicked off, Julián started on the bench, replacing Erling for the last twenty minutes of most matches. He didn't want to go back to being a super sub again, but it was fine… for now. At City, very few players became superstars straight away because Pep preferred to ease them into the team slowly. Plus, the manager had plenty of other amazing attacking options to choose from.

So there was no need for Julián to panic. It was still early days at one of the world's biggest clubs, and he was still adapting to the style of English football. The game was so fast and physical that he hardly had any time on the ball. So, what runs and movements could he make to create a bit more space for himself?

That's what Julián was busy working on in training. He was eager to improve as quickly as possible, and what better place to learn than at City under Pep, and alongside so many world-class superstars? Then, when he got his next chance, he just had to be alert and ready to take it...

After weeks of patient progress, Julián finally got to play together with Erling as a proper strike partnership, and wow, what a performance! In the first half against Nottingham Forest, Erling scored a hat-trick, and in the second, it was Julián's turn to shine. Racing onto Riyad's flick-on, he steadied himself and then swept the ball past the keeper.

*Gooooooooooooooooooooaaaaaaaaaaaaaaaaalllllllllllllll llllllllllll!!!!!!!!!!!!!!!!!!!*

'Great strike, Juli!' Erling cheered, giving him a big hug.

And the Argentinian wasn't done. Before the final whistle blew, Julián added a second goal, this time with a powerful swing of his weaker left foot. 6–0! Watching on the sidelines, Pep clapped and smiled. City's new strikers were looking lethal already.

For their next Premier League match against Aston Villa, however, Julián was back on the City bench, and that's where he mostly stayed. As a late sub, he was struggling to make an impact, but when he got to play from the start? That was a different story.

Julián burst into the six-yard box to score his first Champions League goal against Copenhagen. *GOAL!*

A few games later, he split the Sevilla defence with a clever ball to Rico Lewis. *ASSIST!*

Then, running onto a Kevin master-pass, he rounded the keeper and scored one of his own. *GOAL!*

A few days later, in the Premier League against Fulham, he spun away from his marker and blasted the ball in off the crossbar. *GOAL!*

And a few days after that in the EFL Cup against Chelsea, he scored again with a tap-in at the back post. *GOAL!*

Three goals in three games! 'Come onnnnnn!' Julián cried out, as his teammates hugged and high-fived him. Week by week, game by game, and goal by goal, he was getting used to his new life in England. His brothers were now playing for local non-league club Abbey Hey, and he was really settling in at City.

Just as Julián found his best form again, however,

the club season stopped for a six-week break; the 2022 FIFA World Cup was taking place in Qatar. France and Brazil were the tournament favourites, but Messi's Argentina were on a mission to win it, and Julián couldn't wait to play his part.

## CHAPTER 21

# 2022 WORLD CUP PART 1: FROM THE BENCH TO THE BIG-TIME

Aged twenty-two, Julián was about to fulfil his childhood dream of playing in a World Cup! When he heard the great news that he was going to Qatar, he felt proud and excited, but not surprised. No, he had worked hard to earn his place in the squad.

Since making his international debut against Chile back in June 2021, Julián had become a regular member of Scaloni's very successful Argentina side. So far, he had mostly been used as a sub:

At the Copa América, which they had won,

In the World Cup qualifiers, during which they hadn't lost a single match,

And in the Finalissima, where they had beaten Italy

3–0 to lift another trophy.

What a team – Argentina were now unbeaten in thirty-six matches! Julián, however, was hungry for more game-time, and as the World Cup approached, that second striker spot alongside Messi was still up for grabs.

Lautaro Martínez was Scaloni's first choice for now, but just like at City, whenever Julián got the chance to start, he took it superbly. He had scored his first Argentina goal in their last World Cup qualifier against Ecuador, and he scored in each of their last two World Cup warm-up matches too.

Against Jamaica, Julián calmly guided Lautaro's cross past the keeper. *GOAL!*

And against UAE, he burst forward to finish off one of Messi's magical solo runs. *GOAL!*

'Well done, Juli!' Lionel cheered happily as they high-fived together.

Lionel's intelligence and skill, combined with Julián's energy and speed – they looked like a perfect partnership, but would they be Argentina's World Cup strikeforce?

No, for their first group game against Saudi Arabia, Scaloni picked Lautaro to start alongside Lionel, instead of Julián. Oh well, never mind, there would be more matches, and he was there to help his country in whatever way he could. If that meant supporting his teammates from the bench – and hopefully coming on as a super sub – then sure, no problem!

*Vamos Argentina!*

With Julián cheering them on from the sidelines, his teammates got off to the perfect start. After a foul in the penalty area, Lionel stepped up and calmly scored from the spot. It was 1–0, and they hadn't even played ten minutes!

But if Argentina thought they were going to cruise to an easy victory, they thought wrong. At half-time, it was still only 1–0, and after the break, Saudi Arabia came out fighting. In five mad minutes, they scored twice to take the lead!

Woah, what on earth was going on? Soon after the second goal, Scaloni decided to make a double substitution:

Enzo on for Leandro Paredes,

And Julián on for Papu Gómez.

This was it; Julián's chance to save the day for Argentina on his World Cup debut! Julián raced around the pitch trying to get on the ball, but despite his best efforts, it kept flying past him, over him, or just behind him.

Julián didn't give up, though, and he never stopped running. At last, in the ninetieth minute, a golden chance arrived. The Saudi Arabia keeper punched a cross away and the ball bounced down to Julián inside the box. In a flash, he pulled his leg back and blasted a shot at goal, but a defender managed to clear it off the line.

'Noooooooooo!' Julián groaned, throwing his head back in disappointment. So close to saving the day! Moments later, the final whistle blew. Argentina 1 Saudi Arabia 2 – their World Cup was off to the worst possible start.

Julián and his teammates trudged off the pitch looking miserable, but they needed to pick themselves up quickly and prepare for their next match against Mexico. Argentina had to win, otherwise they would be heading home early.

After sixty minutes against Mexico, the score was still 0–0, so again, Scaloni turned to his subs. This time, he brought Julián on for Lautaro, to play alongside Messi as a second striker. And Argentina's new strikeforce made a difference straight away.

When Lionel controlled a pass from Ángel just outside the box, *ZOOM!* Julián was off, making a clever run between the centre-backs. As the space opened up, however, Lionel had a much better idea: a powerful low shot into the bottom corner. *1–0!*

'Yesssssssssss!' Julián screamed as he chased after Lionel. What a relief! Argentina were winning at last, and their other super sub, Enzo, scored a late second goal to secure the victory.

Phew, first must-win match: won! Now, if they could just beat Poland, they would make it through to the knock-out rounds.

'Let's keep shouting, keep believing, keep trusting that in the end we will win,' Julián wrote to his fans on social media. 'Let's show the world that together we can. Vamos Argentina!'

His days of supporting his teammates from the sidelines, however, were over. After their impressive performances against Mexico, Scaloni decided that it was time to move Julián and Enzo into the starting line-up. So, could they inspire their team to victory again?

Even when Lionel missed a penalty, Argentina kept believing and they kept attacking, until at last the goals arrived. Early in the second half, Alexis Mac Allister raced on to a cross from right-back Nahuel Molina and swept the ball in off the post. *1–0!*

Yessss, the breakthrough they had been waiting for! Now, could Argentina score again to really settle the nerves of all the supporters?

In the sixty-sixth minute, Enzo dribbled forward and then fed the ball to Julián as he entered the box. He had a defender marking him closely, but Julián used his strength and skilful feet to create just enough space to… *BANG!* fire an unstoppable shot into the top corner of the net. *2–0!*

*Goooooooooooooooooooooaaaaaaaaaaaaaaaaalllllllllllllll lllllllllll!!!!!!!!!!!!!!!!!!!!*

What a strike! With his arms out wide and a huge smile across his face, Julián raced over towards the fans, together with Enzo, his friend and old River Plate teammate. They weren't World Cup super-subs anymore; they were World Cup super-STARTERS!

*VAMOOOOOOOOOOOOS!*

'First goal accomplished,' Julián posted later that night. 'Let's go for more.'

After their awful start against Saudi Arabia, Argentina had bounced back to find their best team and their best form. Suddenly, with Enzo in midfield and Julián playing alongside Lionel in attack, they looked unstoppable again.

## CHAPTER 22

# 2022 WORLD CUP PART 2: CHAMPIONS OF THE WORLD!

In the World Cup Round of 16, Argentina battled their way past Australia, and who scored the goals? Their new superstar strikeforce!

First, in a crowded penalty area, Lionel somehow slotted the ball through a defender's legs and around the keeper. It was 1–0 – a moment of Messi magic!

'Yesssssss!' cried Julián as he jumped on Lionel's back.

Then, twenty minutes later, Julián raced across the pitch to close the keeper down, stole the ball off him, and scored into an empty net. It was 2–0 – a moment of Álvarez aggression!

'Yesssssss!' cried Lionel as he jumped into

Julián's arms.

Once upon a time, Messi had been Julián's hero, but now they were partners on the pitch, and they seemed perfect for each other.

The Argentina players weren't getting carried away, though. 'Another small step' – that's what Julián called it. They still had a long way to go, starting with a tough quarter-final against the Netherlands.

When a tired Julián was taken off in the eighty-second minute, there only looked like one possible winner: Argentina. They were 2–0 up, thanks to a goal and an amazing assist from Lionel. So, game over? No, all of a sudden, the Netherlands came alive, and Argentina fell apart.

*2–1... 2–2!*

Uh-oh, the game was going to extra-time, and then to... penalties! Sitting on the subs bench, Julián could hardly bear to watch, but he never stopped believing in his team. Lionel, Lautaro, Enzo – they were all excellent penalty takers, and their keeper, Emi Martínez, was the best in the business when it came to spot-kicks.

*Vamos Argentina!*

When Emi saved the first two Dutch penalties, Julián did breathe a sigh of relief, but he only fully relaxed once the whole thing was over and Argentina were the winners.

'You did it – we did it!' Julián cheered as he hugged each of the heroes: Lautaro, who had scored the winning spot-kick, then Lionel, and then Emi. Hurray, Argentina were through to the World Cup semi-finals!

'Olé, olé, olé, ola!' the whole squad sang together as they jumped up and down in front of their supporters. Their team spirit was stronger than ever.

What a night, and there were even bigger celebrations ahead, especially for Julián...

In the semi-finals against Croatia, Argentina were the team on top again, but this time, they didn't look back or lose their nerve. And it wasn't Lionel who led the way in the Lusail Iconic Stadium; it was his young striker partner.

*ZOOM!* Julián raced onto Enzo's through-ball, but as he went to shoot, the Croatia keeper fouled him. Penalty! Up stepped Lionel to score from the spot. *1–0!*

Then five minutes later, *ZOOM!* Julián was off again, dribbling with skill and determination all the way from the halfway line to the six-yard box, before finishing with a volley. *2–0!*

*Gooooooooooooooooooooaaaaaaaaaaaaaaaallllllllllllll llllllllllll!!!!!!!!!!!!!!!!!!!!*

Wow, what a sensational run – Julián was definitely a World Cup superstar now! As he shared a hug with Lionel, he listened to the fans clapping, cheering and chanting his name.

*ÁLVAREZ! ÁLVAREZ! ÁLVAREZ!*

Unbelievable! It was a moment that Julián would never forget, but he didn't stop there. No, he never stopped and he always wanted more.

Midway through the second half, he sprinted forward to support Messi on one of his magical solo runs. Eventually, Lionel twisted and turned away from his marker and cut the ball back to the edge of the six-yard box, where Julián was waiting to score his fourth goal of the tournament. *3–0!*

Game over? It really was – Argentina were through

to the World Cup final! Soon it was time for the players to get the party started again...

*Olé, olé, olé, ola!*

*Vamos, vamos Argentina!*

The next day, however, it was straight back to the training field for Julián and his teammates. The trophy wasn't theirs yet, and they still had lots of work to do. As the big final approached, Julián sent a message to his fans, along with a photo of the whole, happy squad:

'The last small step, EVERYONE TOGETHER!'

It was all set to be a sensational end to the 2022 World Cup – Argentina versus the reigning champions, France. Most people were talking about the battle between Messi and Kylian Mbappé, but they would be far from the only superstars out on the pitch:

Emi, Raphaël Varane, Enzo, Antoine Griezmann, Ángel, Olivier Giroud... and Julián, of course!

Julián was full of confidence after his semi-final performance, and determined to continue shining brightly on football's biggest stage. So what if it was a World Cup final? With one of his very first touches of the game, Julián played a cheeky back-heel to Alexis, who shot straight at the France keeper. *Unlucky!*

Argentina were looking dangerous every time they attacked. In the twentieth minute, Lionel played the ball to Julián, who poked a clever first-time pass over to Ángel on the left wing. Ángel faked to cross, and then cut inside, into the box, where he was fouled by Ousmane Dembélé. *Penalty!*

Lionel ran up and... sent the keeper the wrong way. *1–0 to Argentina!*

As their captain slid across the grass, Julián and the other players piled on top of him. They had scored the first goal of the final, and it felt like a massive moment.

Fifteen minutes later, Argentina were celebrating again. Alexis swept the ball forward to Lionel, who flicked it to Julián on the right wing, who played it through for Alexis, who was bursting through the middle.

'Go on, go on!' the fans urged, rising to their feet in anticipation. Their team was playing brilliantly – what a goal this would be!

As he chased after the ball, Alexis looked across and

spotted Ángel racing up the left wing in loads of space. So he played the pass, and let Ángel get the glory. *2–0!*

Argentina's attackers ran around screaming like little kids in the playground, eyes wide with disbelief – what a terrific team goal, they were in dreamland!

With fifteen minutes to go, Argentina were still 2–0 up and cruising to the World Cup trophy, but that's when Mbappé decided to show that anything Messi could do, he could do too.

First, he scored from the penalty spot, and then a minute later, he scored again with a stunning slide volley. *2–2!*

No way, it was like the Netherlands match all over again! The Argentina players were stunned, but they had come too far together to give up now.

'Come on, we can still win this!' Julián roared to his teammates when he was taken off in extra-time. All he could do now was cheer his brothers on in the penalty shoot-out.

*Yesssssss!* Emi dived down low to save from Kingsley Coman.

*Yesssssss!* Paulo Dybala scored.

*Yesssssss!* Emi outfoxed France midfielder Aurélien Tchouaméni, who dragged his shot wide.

*Yesssssss!* Leandro Paredes scored. Wow, they were so close now. Moments later, Julián's old River teammate Gonzalo Montiel was walking forward with the chance to win it for Argentina. After a slow run-up, he… scored!

*VAMOOOOOOOOOOOOOOSSSSSSSSSSSSS!*

It was all over – Argentina had won the World Cup, they were the new Champions of the World! In his excitement, Julián didn't know who to hug first: Emi or Gonzalo, Enzo or Lionel?

'We did it, we did it!' he cried again and again, as his smile grew wider and wider and tears ran down his cheeks.

What an incredible and emotional journey it had been for all them, but especially for Julián. From the subs bench, he had forced his way into the Argentina starting line-up, and then into a starring role alongside Lionel and Ángel in attack. With four goals, he had even finished as the tournament's third highest scorer!

But really, Julián wasn't so interested in the

individual stats. What mattered most was the team achievements, and his team had just won the biggest football trophy of them all: the World Cup. And it was almost time to collect it.

With his winner's medal around his neck, Julián walked up onto the stage, but on his way, he couldn't help stopping to give the famous gold trophy a quick kiss. Mwah, what a beauty! He was looking forward to lifting it high into the sky, but first, it was Lionel's turn as captain...

*3... 2... 1...*

*Hurrrrrrraaaaaaaaaaaaayyyy!*

*Olé, olé, olé, ola!*

*Vamos, vamos Argentina!*

*Dale campeón, dale campeón...*

## CHAPTER 23

# TREBLE SUCCESS WITH CITY

The World Cup celebrations went on and on, first in Qatar and then back in Argentina, where they returned home as heroes. Even though their flight arrived at three in the morning, there were still thousands of fans waiting at the airport to greet them, plus an open-top bus with three words written on it in huge letters:

'*Campeones Del Mundo*': 'Champions of the World'.

Later that day, the Argentina players went on a victory parade around Buenos Aires, and found over four million people partying in the streets!

'This is crazy!' Julián said to Enzo, while they posed for yet more photos together with the trophy.

Eventually, however, it was time for Julián to get back to playing football and back to Manchester City. His club needed him to help them win more trophies!

As the season restarted in late December, City were still fighting hard in four different competitions: the EFL Cup, the Premier League, the FA Cup and the Champions League. No English club had every won a Quadruple before, but could they be the first to do it? Why not?! Julián and his teammates were aiming to win as many trophies as possible…

*1) The EFL Cup?*

Unfortunately, not; City failed to win their fifth EFL Cup trophy in a row. After battling past Liverpool in the fourth round, they suffered a shock defeat to Southampton in the quarter-finals.

'Nooooooo!' Julián groaned as the final whistle blew. For once, Pep had picked him to play as the team's central striker, which meant it was his job to score. That job became even more important when Saints took a 2–0 lead, but with the pressure on, Julián had missed two of City's biggest chances:

A slide finish in the six-yard box that only trickled

off his boot,

And the best of all, a one-on-one with the keeper, where his shot flew just wide of the far post.

'Arghh, I should be scoring that!' Julián screamed, burying his face in his hands. Even when Erling came on in the second half, he couldn't turn things around for City.

Oh well, it was just one bad game in a long, hard season. After a miserable journey back to Manchester, it was time to move straight on. Goodbye, Quadruple; hello Treble. City had already won a domestic treble in 2019 (the Premier League, plus the two English cups), but a continental one – including a European trophy – was even harder to achieve. No English team had won one of those since Manchester United in 1999...

*2) The Premier League?*

At the beginning of 2023, City were second in the table, seven points behind Arsenal, but the team always believed that they could turn things around and lift the trophy again. And that's exactly what they did, winning sixteen of their next eighteen matches, including a remarkable run of twelve wins in a row.

It was an unbelievable effort from every single City player. While Erling was definitely the main man up front, Julián was determined to be more than just the back-up striker. He was a World Cup winner now, and he was eager to play as many games and score as many goals as possible. And that's exactly what he did, often as a second striker alongside Erling:

*BANG!* Julián pounced on a loose ball in the box to launch an amazing City fightback against Tottenham.

*TAP!* He stayed calm and scored a crucial equaliser against Liverpool.

*SMASH!* He curled a sensational, long-range shot into the top corner to win the game against Fulham.

*Goooooooooooooooooooaaaaaaaaaaaaaaaalllllllllllllll llllllllllll!!!!!!!!!!!!!!!!!!!!*

'Vamoooooooos!' Julián roared, leaping up and punching the air. He was starting to perform like a real Premier League superstar now, and afterwards, his manager was full of praise.

'He's an incredible, exceptional player,' Pep said with a proud smile.

West Ham, Leeds, Everton – with each win, City

got closer and closer to the trophy, until all they needed was one more victory, or one more Arsenal defeat, and the title would be theirs. As it turned out, both of those things arrived on the same weekend. First, Arsenal lost to Nottingham Forest and then the next day, City beat Chelsea. And who scored their winning goal again?

Yes, Julián! So what if they had already won the league? He never stopped running, and he was always hungry for more. In the twelfth minute, he raced forward, controlled a pass from Cole Palmer, and calmly fired a shot past the keeper. *1–0!*

*Gooooooooooooooooooooaaaaaaaaaaaaaaaaalllllllllllllll llllllllllll!!!!!!!!!!!!!!!!!!!*

It was Julián's ninth league strike of the season, and he had only started twelve games. Touch, bang, goal – he was making scoring for Manchester City look so easy now. And once the match was won, it was trophy time…

*3… 2… 1…*

*Hurrrraaaaaaaaaaaaaayyyyy!*

*Campeones, Campeones, Olé! Olé! Olé!*

One trophy successfully lifted, but would there be more to come that season? Julián certainly hoped so because City still had two epic cup finals ahead of them.

*3) The FA Cup?*

First up: the FA Cup final against their massive Manchester rivals, United. Julián had scored against Chelsea and Burnley in the earlier rounds, but for the biggest game of all, Pep picked Kevin De Bruyne and İlkay Gündoğan to play behind Erling in attack.

As he took his seat on the City subs bench, Julián was disappointed, of course, but it turned out to be a brilliant decision because İlkay scored two goals and Kevin set them both up.

'Yesssssssssssss!' Julián jumped up and cheered.

Whether they were on the pitch or on the bench, they were all in it together. So when the final whistle blew and City were the winners, Julián raced around celebrating like everyone else.

*Campeones, Campeones, Olé! Olé! Olé!*

Two trophies won, one final still to come. A stunning continental treble was still on...

## 4) The Champions League?

After a painful 1–0 defeat to Chelsea in 2021, City were back in the Champions League final again and their players were absolutely determined to lift the trophy this time. So, what would the line-up be for their last and biggest game of the season against Italians Inter Milan? Although he had scored a last-minute goal in the semi-final against Real Madrid, Julián wasn't surprised to hear that he would be starting on the bench.

'But hopefully, I'll still have a part to play!' he thought positively.

The first half ticked by without a goal, and so did the first twenty minutes of the second half. As he watched, Julián's legs grew more and more restless, and his eyes kept turning to his manager.

'Please Pep, put me on!' he wanted to shout, but just when it looked like City might call for a super sub, they scored. Bernardo burst into the box and pulled the ball back to Rodri, who coolly placed a shot in the bottom corner. *1–0!*

Yesssssss, at last! While Rodri and the other City

starters went wild on the pitch, Julián shared a hug with the other subs on the sidelines. They were all in it together, and they were now less than thirty minutes away from lifting the one trophy the club had been waiting years for...

'Keep going, guys!' Julián urged his teammates on, and when the final whistle blew and City were the winners, he raced around celebrating like everyone else.

*Campeones, Campeones, Olé! Olé! Olé!*

Hurray, they had done it! City had completed the Treble, and for Julián, it was really a Quadruple because he had won the World Cup too. What a season it had been for him in 2022–23: sixty games played, twenty-three goals scored, and four major trophies lifted! A record-breaking season, in fact, because Julián had become the first player to ever win the World Cup and a continental treble in the same season.

'Thank you all so much for your love and support,' he wrote to his followers, with a picture of him proudly wearing all four gold medals at the same time.

'Now, for a little rest.'

After such an amazing year for club and country, would Julián slow down and just enjoy his success for a while? No way, he was still the same Little Spider of Calchín – always humble, always hard-working, and always hungry for more. So, as soon as the 2023–24 season started, *ZOOM!* Julián was off again, racing around the pitch, scoring and setting up lots more goals for Manchester City.

**ÁLVAREZ HONOURS**

## River Plate

🏆 Copa Libertadores: 2018

🏆 Copa Argentina: 2018–19

🏆 Supercopa Argentina: 2019

🏆 Argentine Primera División: 2021

## Manchester City

🏆 Premier League: 2022–23

🏆 FA Cup: 2022–23

🏆 UEFA Champions League: 2022–23

🏆 UEFA Super Cup: 2023

## Argentina

🏆 Copa América: 2021

🏆 CONMEBOL–UEFA Cup of Champions (the 'Finalissima'): 2022

🏆 FIFA World Cup: 2022

## Individual

🏆 Argentine Primera División top scorer: 2021

🏆 South American Footballer of the Year: 2021

# ÁLVAREZ

## 19 THE FACTS

**NAME:** Julián Álvarez

**DATE OF BIRTH:** 31 January 2000

**PLACE OF BIRTH:** Calchín

**NATIONALITY:** Argentina

**BEST FRIENDS:** Brothers Rafael and Agustin

**CURRENT CLUB:** Manchester City

**POSITION:** ST

## THE STATS

| | |
|---|---|
| Height (cm): | 170 |
| Club appearances: | 185 |
| Club goals: | 78 |
| Club trophies: | 8 |
| International appearances: | 26 |
| International goals: | 7 |
| International trophies: | 3 |
| Ballon d'Ors: | 0 |

★ ★ ★ HERO RATING: 87 ★ ★ ★

# GREATEST MOMENTS

## 9 DECEMBER 2018,
## RIVER PLATE 3–1 BOCA JUNIORS

As an eighteen-year-old rising star, Julián only played the last twenty-five minutes of this massive Copa Libertadores final, but that was enough time to play his part and make a difference. With his energy, talent and determination, Julián helped set up his team's second goal and then defended bravely to help River Plate beat their fierce rivals Boca Juniors. It was the first of many big-game performances.

## 3 OCTOBER 2021, RIVER PLATE 2–1 BOCA JUNIORS

Nearly three years later, Julián took on Boca again, but this time, as River's superstar striker. In the Superclásico, the fans were expecting him to do something special, and he did. First, he dribbled past two defenders and scored with a sensational strike from thirty yards out, and then Julián added a second goal to seal an important win on River's path to becoming Champions of Argentina.

## 25 MAY 2022, RIVER PLATE 8–1 ALIANZA LIMA

Back at River Plate for a last six-month loan, Julián was determined to say goodbye in style. And what better way to do that and also say 'See you soon, Manchester City!' than scoring six goals in one single game? In this Copa Libertadores match, Julián completed his first hat-trick before half-time, and scored his second with ten minutes to spare. Yes, City had signed a superstar!

## DECEMBER 2022,
## ARGENTINA 3–0 CROATIA

Julián forced his way into Argentina's starting World Cup line-up, and in the semi-final against Croatia, took on a starring role alongside his hero Lionel Messi. Julián used his power, speed and skill to win a penalty for his team and then score two goals of his own, leading them to the final against France, where Argentina were crowned Champions of the World.

## 30 APRIL 2023,
## FULHAM 1–2 MANCHESTER CITY

In his first EPL season, Julián got better and better with every game. Against Fulham, he played as a second striker behind Erling Haaland, but Julián played the starring role. After winning the penalty that led to the first goal, he then scored the second himself with a curling, long-range shot into the top corner. Just weeks later, City won the league title, on their way to an incredible continental treble.

# TEST YOUR KNOWLEDGE

## QUESTIONS

1. Who gave Julián the nickname 'the Little Spider'?

2. Which big European club did Julián almost join at the age of eleven?

3. Who was Julián's ultimate childhood football hero?

4. How old was Julián when he finally signed for River Plate?

5. True or false – Julián won the Copa Libertadores at the age of eighteen?

**6.** What two things did Julián give to his old Atlético Calchín coach, Rafael Varas?

**7.** Julián was top scorer in the Argentine Primera División when River Plate were crowned Champions in 2021. How many league goals did he score that season?

**8.** Which Argentina striker helped persuade Julián to move to Manchester City?

**9.** Which other young striker joined Julián at Manchester City for the 2022–23 season?

**10.** How many goals did Julián score for Argentina at the 2022 FIFA World Cup?

**11.** How many trophies did Julián win during the 2022–23 season, for club and country?

Answers below . . . No cheating!

*1. His brothers Rafael and Agustín. 2. Real Madrid. 3. Lionel Messi. 4. Sixteen. 5. True! 6. A signed River Plate shirt and a new van. 7. Eighteen. 8. Sergio Agüero. 9. Erling Haaland. 10. Four. 11. Four.*

# PLAY LIKE YOUR HEROES

## HOW TO PRESS FROM THE FRONT LIKE JULIÁN ÁLVAREZ

Winning is one big team effort, and that means everyone has to work really hard, even superstar strikers like you. Yes, your main job is to attack and score, but you also need to do your bit in defence. So, whenever the other team has the ball, think of it as a race to win the ball back as quickly as possible.

**STEP 1:** If a defender or goalkeeper is taking a long time on the ball, ZOOM! Rush forward to close them down and put them under pressure, so they suddenly think, 'Arggh, what am I going to do now?!' Go it alone if you have to, but the best teams press together.

**STEP 2:** If the player goes for a big, hurried hoof, be brave and try to block it.

**STEP 3:** If the player goes for a panicky pass, be smart and try to predict where it will go, stretching out your leg to intercept it.

**STEP 4:** If the player goes for a dodgy dribble, be careful and try to tackle them without committing a foul.

**STEP 5:** Well done! You've successfully won the ball back, and the best thing about pressing from the front is that you're further forward, much closer to the opposition goal. You've done the hard work; now, you've just got to stay calm and score...

**STEP 6:** GOAL! You're the hero, but don't forget to celebrate with all your friends. Remember, winning is one big team effort.

## CAN'T GET ENOUGH OF
# ULTIMATE FOOTBALL HEROES?

Check out heroesfootball.com
for quizzes, games, and competitions!

Plus join the Ultimate Football Heroes
Fan Club to score exclusive content and
be the first to hear about
new books and events.
heroesfootball.com/subscribe/